## Pra… …yles' … …re

"This seemingly simple story touched m… …so loved how Ben's insecurities were portrayed … …eetly his crush on Ollie is depicted. I just liked both … …n pretty much almost as soon as they appeared on … pages... Highly recommended."

~ *Reviews by Jessewave*

"...Josephine Myles has amazing storytelli… …so has a knack for making you fall in … characters...and makes you want to root for … right way for them at least once in their l… …ing a good book needs- humor, romance and lot… ."

~ *Night Owl Reviews*

"This is the second book I've read from Josephine Myles, and I will definitely be hitting up her back list at this point."

~ *Fiction Vixen*

"Handle with Care by Josephine Myles is a really sweet story... Ms. Myles is a good author and I really enjoy her style. I look forward to her next tale of quirky English boys and the guys they find to love!"

~ *Guilty Pleas…*

Look for these titles by

*Josephine Myles*

*Now Available:*

Barging In

Handle with Care

The Hot Floor

# Handle with Care

*Josephine Myles*

SAMHAIN
PUBLISHING

Samhain Publishing, Ltd.
11821 Mason Montgomery Road, 4B
Cincinnati, OH 45249
www.samhainpublishing.com

Handle with Care

Print ISBN: 978-1-61921-114-8
Digital ISBN: 978-1-60928-965-2



Editing by Linda Ingmanson
Cover by Kanaxa



First Samhain Publishing, Ltd. electronic publication: April 2012
First Samhain Publishing, Ltd. print publication: March 2013

# Dedication

For Graham, my long suffering "houseboy".

Also, thanks to Lou, for reading through the first draft and giving me plenty of encouragement along the way; to Jamie for her spot-on critique; to Krista for going through all the medical details and reassuring me I had them right; and to my team of wonderful beta readers: Don, Blaine, Susan, JRose, Kaje, and Jennifer.

# Chapter One

"Oh my God, Benji, are you planning on opening some kind of gay porn lending library?" Zoe's voice carried through from my bedroom to my office and roused me from my coding-induced trance. I flushed.

"Oi! You're meant to be cleaning, not snooping."

Zoe stuck her head around the door and smirked at me. "Just thought the contents of your cupboard could do with a dusting." She held up a box: *Gay Gladiator: He will bring them cock, and they will love him for it*. "This one looks interesting. Mind if I borrow it?"

"It doesn't actually have Russell Crowe in it, if that's what you're hoping. And there's not much of a plot that I can recall."

"Does it need a plot with all those hot men in it?"

God, she really did look interested. I wasn't about to lend porn to my sister, though. That would just be...disturbing. I got up and swiped the box from her hand, then tapped her on the head with it.

"It's not for you, little sis. Besides which, it wasn't all that good." It was one I'd bought in one of my early, indiscriminate buying sprees. I was getting far more selective these days and trying to seek out films with the kind of guys I really went for. Problem was, there weren't all that many pornos out there featuring cute, skate-punk delivery guys with purple hair. Okay, I tell a lie; there were none. I had to make do with my own imagination for those fantasies.

God, what was I going to do for kicks if I lost interest in the films? A man needs some kind of vice, and since the kidney failure, I'd been banned from practically everything else that was bad for me. I really, really didn't want to have to start gambling. Knowing my luck, I'd end up bankrupt and homeless, and seeing as how my home and income were about the only things I had left going for me, the thought of losing them brought me out in a cold sweat.

The doorbell chimed, and I jumped. I glanced out the window and spotted my favourite yellow van outside. The driver was out of sight, hidden down the side of the house where the front door opened onto the driveway.

"It's okay, I'll get it," Zoe said, already on her way to the door.

"No! I've got it." I pushed past her and practically ran down the hallway. That familiar, purple-crested, green shape waited behind the frosted glass.

"Hey there," I said as I opened the door, vainly trying to suppress my panting. Damn, I was so unfit. I tried to get in some daily exercise with my Wii and my rowing machine, but I tired so quickly these days. "Great to see you." Oh God, I sounded so fucking desperate. I tried to rein it back in. "You have something for me?" I was trying to remember if I was due a DVD today.

Ollie had tufty purple hair, big brown eyes, and one of those weird piercings that went through the top part of his ear twice. That combination of punk and cute always gets me, and he was cuter than a Manga-style kitten.

"Hey, Ben," he said, beaming at me like I was an old friend

rather than just the weird recluse on his delivery round with the three-DVD-a-day habit. His smile revealed that gap between his front teeth, and I couldn't help staring at it. What should have been a flaw only made him more bloody adorable. "How's things?"

"Yeah, not so bad." I sounded croaky and had to cough to clear my throat. God, I must have looked like I was on death's door. Mind you, I suppose I was. It was only the dialysis keeping me going.

He was still smiling, but there was a trace of concern in his eyes. I tried not to look into them—can't stand being pitied—so I ran a furtive gaze down his body instead. That was probably a mistake, but you can't blame a guy for looking. I might not have been in a fit state to go out on the pull anymore, but I still had twenty-twenty vision and a vivid imagination. It was currently working overtime trying to strip Ollie's uniform off him. Somehow, he always managed to make the forest-green polyester look sexy.

Ollie was slight, and I dwarfed him by at least six inches, but he gave that impression of barely restrained energy like smaller guys often do. The shirt fit him well, hugging his lean body. I could see part of a tattoo peeking out from under a sleeve but was distracted from trying to decipher it by the ropey muscle and dark hair of his forearms. His trousers were baggy and frayed at the heel, with one of those long key chains hanging down over one thigh, and his black boots had chunky soles. The skate-punk stylings made him look like he was barely old enough to buy cigarettes, and I was starting to feel like a dirty old man for lusting after him.

"Looks like another DVD today. You watch more films than anyone I know." He held the scanner out to me while I struggled with the fiddly little stylus and attempted to create something like my usual signature on the slippery screen. It was even harder to focus because I could see him straining to peer around me and was suddenly paranoid that I'd left something embarrassing on view in the hallway. I had to fight the urge to look around and check.

It wasn't like there'd be anything that incriminating, after all. There was a stack of boxes full of the next month's dialysate bags, but Ollie wouldn't know what they were, and I was fairly sure I wouldn't have had cause to leave a porn magazine in view. I don't tend to wank in the hallway. Actually, I've never wanked in the hallway. Maybe I should try it sometime; I was all for infusing a little variety into my solitary sex life. It would probably be more of a novelty than the contents of the parcel Ollie had tucked under his arm, after all. Best not to think about that, though. Not right now with the smell of his spicy-sweet aftershave tickling my nose and his hands only inches from mine.

"You know, you've got a great place here. Is it all yours?" Ollie wasn't bothering to hide the fact that he was openly checking out my hallway.

"Yeah, but just the ground floor. Bought it before the property market went mental." I'd been lucky, because even a year later, there was no way I'd have been able to afford it on my beginner's salary. Money had been tight for the first few years, but it'd been worth it to be able to bring Zoe up in a pleasant neighbourhood of Victorian, red-brick semis in a quiet part of Reading. They were all large houses, and my flat had two good-sized bedrooms at the front, with the kitchen and living room opening onto a sunny courtyard at the back. My bathroom was a windowless afterthought crammed in at the end of the hallway, but I'd kitted it out with as much loving attention as the rest of the rooms.

Thirteen years and a river of sweat and tears later, the place was looking pretty damn good inside and out. Every room was tastefully restored to retain the period features, but with modern furnishings in carefully coordinated, muted colours. Great. Now even my house was better looking than I was.

"Mind if I poke my head in?"

"Uh, yeah. Okay." Shit, why did he have to suggest that when Zoe was sitting in the kitchen, no doubt listening to every word? I could have invited Ollie in for a coffee if it were just me.

Who was I fooling? There's no way I'd have risked being shot down by him. Much better to have at least the vaguest hope in my head than to know for sure he thought I was a creep.

"Hey, nice key holder."

Oh God, I'd forgotten all about that. My one piece of tasteless kitsch; it would have to be the first thing he noticed, wouldn't it? It was a life-size cardboard cut-out of Alan Cumming as Nightcrawler in the second X-Men film. I'd put nails through the card and hung my keys off them so it looked like he was carrying them. I might as well have put a sign up proclaiming "nerd in residence".

"Good choice. He's my all-time favourite X-Men character. I mean, Wolverine's pretty cool and all, but Nightcrawler has style. I was gutted when they killed him off." Ollie pouted a little at the thought.

I must have looked as confused as I felt, because he grinned again. "Sorry, you probably haven't read the comics. I've got a bit of a collection, but I guess most people only know the films."

I bristled at the implication that I was one of the ignorant masses but realised from Ollie's guileless expression that he probably hadn't meant it to sound like that. "I have a few of the graphic novels, but I didn't know they'd killed him off."

"Yeah, it's in *Second Coming,* if you want to check it out. At least they gave him a decent death n' all, but I was really pissed off about it. Still"—that quicksilver grin was back—"there's all the alternate universe versions, and I'm sure there'll be more. They just like to keep going with these things."

"Right. Of course." I wasn't sure if I could keep up with this conversation, but I enjoyed watching the rapid play of emotions over Ollie's face.

I realised I was staring when he gave me a quizzical look followed by a flash of something knowing in his eyes.

"Time to love you and leave you."

*If only.* I could have done with a little loving, even if he did leave straight after.

Ollie grinned again and thrust the parcel in my direction. "See you tomorrow, yeah? I expect I'll have something for you." He raised his eyebrows, and the smile got even broader. "I usually do."

That had to be just common courtesy, right? That and a friendly feeling because we liked the same fictional character. The idea of there being anything more behind his words and warm smile was ridiculous and not the sort of thing someone in my condition should be thinking about. Besides, my gaydar had always been rubbish—the only place I'd ever plucked up the courage to approach guys was in gay bars, and even then I'd needed some chemical courage buzzing through my veins to act the part of predatory top.

But those days were over. The strongest substance likely to pass my lips now was a cup of tea, and even those were carefully rationed.

I stuttered a goodbye and tried not to stare at Ollie's arse as he walked back to the van, gravel crunching under his feet.

I didn't succeed.

He swung around as he climbed into the cab, and I swear that he must have caught me ogling him because his grin went impish. He gave me a little wave, casual-like, and I tried to return it in the same spirit. Bet my face gave me away though. When I got back inside and finally looked in the mirror, I'd gone beet-red. I also discovered my hair was doing its best impersonation of a mullet, with the top slicked down with grease and the back fanning out to almost brush my shoulders.

Bugger. I really needed to do something about that.

"Sooo..." A hand landed on my shoulder with some force. "What's going on here, then? Flirting with the delivery guy? Is there something you should be telling me about, Benji?"

The flush on my cheeks gave me away. Damn! I was so busted.

"I wasn't flirting," I said.

Zoe raised her eyebrows. "Yeah, well, you might not have been, but he certainly was."

"You think so?"

"I know so. And it wouldn't have hurt you to reciprocate a bit. He's cute."

I couldn't help the grin that took over my face. "Tell me about it."

Zoe's smile widened. "I knew it! You're into him. Mind you, he's a bit young, isn't he? Can't be older than twenty, I reckon. If that." She pulled a serious face, and I felt like reminding her she was only twenty-one herself, but I bit it back. I'd learnt long ago how much stock she set in seeming mature.

And anyway, I didn't want to discuss Ollie with Zoe. I was the one meant to be interfering in her love life and vetting potential boyfriends—not the other way around. She just seemed to be more interested in her career than in a relationship right now.

"What did you bring me to eat?" I asked her in a transparent attempt to change the subject. Fortunately, food is the one subject guaranteed to distract my pastry-chef sister.

"Come and see." Zoe led the way to the kitchen, and I plodded after her, envying her bouncy gait and boundless energy.

Zoe's twelve years younger than me, and it still came as a surprise sometimes to see her as a grown woman. I carried this picture of her in my heart as a confused and frightened six-year-old, asking her big brother why Mummy and Daddy weren't going to wake up ever again. I had done my best to be a substitute parent for her after the car crash that killed them both, refusing to let her go to a foster home despite the doubts social services had about an eighteen-year-old diabetic acting as her legal guardian.

It was strange having to accept the fact that these days our roles had swapped and she was the one looking after me. It didn't help that she was still so petite. Next to my bulky frame, she looked like another species, but relatives always commented on the fact that we shared Mum's deep blue eyes and thick, dark hair.

I needed to lift my mood. Zoe didn't deserve to be reminded of all that again. I watched her unload her cool-bag into the freezer. "Did you bring me any more of your yummy pasta bakes?"

"Cupboard love, that's all it is with you, isn't it?" Zoe squeezed my arm and smiled.

It turned out there were three tubs of the pasta bake, along with various other homemade treats. It definitely pays to have a sister who's a chef when you're on a severely restricted diet. The sodium content in most ready meals meant there was hardly anything I could eat in the supermarket.

"You're a star, little sis." I pulled her to me and kissed the top of her head.

"Yeah, I know. And one of these days, I'm going to teach you how to cook so I don't have to keep doing this for you."

"Nonsense. You love showing off your skills."

"I love knowing you're eating something tasty." Zoe gave me a long look, and I remembered how, at the age of ten, she taught herself the rudiments of baking just so that there were some decent desserts I could eat. "I don't love cleaning for you, though. You sure you can't afford to hire someone?"

I groaned. Not this conversation again. I felt guilty enough about everything Zoe did for me, but I just didn't have the energy for many chores. "It's not that. I offered to pay you, didn't I? I just don't like the idea of a stranger coming around every day and nosing through my stuff. It's bad enough when it's family." I punched her arm, and she gave me a cheeky grin before pretending to be mortally wounded.

"You wouldn't have to get them in every day, Benji. Just once a week should do it."

"So why do you come round every day?"

"Why do you think, numbskull?" She returned the punch with interest. "Because you're my brother, and for some crazy reason, I care about you. Since you won't take me up on the kidney offer, this is the best I can do, isn't it?"

I closed my eyes on her. It was way too much. I couldn't take a kidney from her. She shouldn't have to physically suffer because of my broken body.

"I think I should wait for a deceased donor," I said as firmly as I could. "It would be better to get a new pancreas at the same time, and you definitely need yours." God, it was like shopping for a two-for-one deal on body parts. Organs-R-Us. I tried not to dwell on the morbidity. On the fact that I was waiting ghoulishly for someone else to die that I might live again.

"I just want to see you get better," she said, her arm snaking around my waist.

"Yeah, I know. Me too." I sighed and rested my chin on her head. I didn't deserve her and I knew it, but I was doing my best to try and be worthy of all that love. I looked down at her and the sensation of my unruly hair flopping down over my forehead reminded me of my resolution to do something about it.

"Hey, Zo, would you mind giving me a quick haircut before you leave? I've still got the clippers."

"What? And ruin that glorious mullet?" Zoe grinned mischievously. "I thought you'd never ask."

# Chapter Two

Three hours after Zoe had left, I hooked up the catheter tube in my belly to an empty bag and started to drain out all the waste dialysis fluid. I'd infused a dialysate bag not long before she'd turned up, so I had to wait for it to diffuse before opening the parcel. It might sound silly, but I had problems getting it up with all the dialysate fluid inside me. I'd look down and see my bloated abdomen and that bloody tube sticking out of me, and any trace of arousal just evaporated. I'd just start thinking about how the fluid was sloshing around inside my peritoneal cavity, getting more and more toxic as it leached all the waste products out of my blood.

In some ways, I'd have preferred to stay on the haemodialysis, which was only three hospital visits a week, but what with the diabetes, it didn't work so well for me. I felt terrible most of the time and kept having crashes. Peritoneal dialysis was better at keeping my blood sugar level, even if it could be a hassle having to infuse and drain four bags a day.

As the fluid drained out, taking all those toxins with it, I ripped open the cardboard wrapper and pulled out the latest acquisition to my library. I was getting quite a collection. Like I said, I had to get the variety somehow, didn't I?

This one promised plenty of XXX action in the jungle, with a bunch of crew-cut, war-painted hunks. The jungle looked suspiciously like a Beverly Hills landscaped garden, but I wasn't about to split hairs over the accuracy of a porn set. Let's face it, no one really cared about the background, right? It was like those old *Star Trek* sets—you ignored the polystyrene boulders and painted sky to concentrate on watching Kirk pace around like a caged tiger. Well, I always had, anyway. The man even managed to make those awful uniforms look sexy.

A bit like a certain delivery courier I could think of.

That odd little sucking sensation I got when the bag was full pulled me back into the present. After I'd unplugged and chucked the sealed bag in the medical waste bin, I took another look at the DVD case. Nope, it just didn't appeal to me at that moment. Seeing those porn stars impersonating soldiers, all I could think about was my new military-style haircut. I ran a hand over my shorn head. Would Ollie even notice it? And if he did, what would he think?

I decided to fill myself up with the next bag and commit to another four hours of looking like a beach ball. I had a conference call due in a couple of hours, but so long as I put on a decent shirt and angled the webcam right, no one could tell I looked any different from how I used to. Except the hair, of course. My boss would probably like that, though.

Turned out he did.

"Afternoon, Ben. You're looking well."

I plastered on a smile. James would never be able to tell how forced it was over the screen. "Feeling great, James. How's the family?"

The family were perfect, as ever. I smiled and nodded and tried to look interested, though, because his kids were cute. The youngest daughter reminded me of Zoe when she was little.

James Littlejohn led a kind of charmed life, it seemed. He'd used his trust fund to set up a financial services software company straight out of business school, and despite not having much computer savvy, he'd surrounded himself with those who had the necessary skills. What's more, he'd managed to keep most of them on with his generous contracts. I certainly wasn't about to argue with my deal, as despite having a serious health condition, I was able to work from home with only a very small slice off my old salary.

"And how's your health?" James asked.

"Oh, can't complain."

"I don't suppose we can ever tempt you back to the workplace? The engineer we've got in now isn't a patch on you. My computer's slowed right down."

I gave a wry grin. "Much as I'd love to help you out, it's not easy while I'm on this dialysis. Believe me, you wouldn't want all my medical equipment littering the break room. I know how you felt when Tamara had her breast-milk pump in there." The look on his face when he'd walked in on her had been priceless. Her expressing milk while I'd been on a break hadn't bothered me, but then again, at the time I'd been in the middle of seeing Zoe through puberty and having to talk with her about periods and safe sex. I think my embarrassment about female matters had long since been overcome.

"No, no, of course. I was forgetting about that." James looked flustered, and I took pity on him.

"When I get a transplant, I'll be right back there, I promise." I said *when*, not *if*, because James didn't need to know the real situation with waiting lists, did he?

It was true, I would have loved to have gone back and resumed tinkering with the computers and not just the code, but I couldn't cope with the idea right now. All those workplace temptations would be torture—everyone drinking coffee and talking about going out and getting drunk. I tried not to think about the state-of-the-art coffeemaker that was gathering dust in my kitchen, because it only made me want to scream with frustration.

"Right. Let's see what we've got for you this week." James shuffled his paper around on his desk. I gave the first genuine smile of our conversation. His reliance on pen and paper in the age of information technology was somehow charming. "We've just started an account with a company called Dane Gibson Associates who need a new integrated payroll system. It's an important account, so I'll need you to check over the work my minions here have been doing."

I listened to James's summary of the new account and tapped out a few relevant notes while simultaneously surfing to DGA's main website to get more of an idea about what I'd be dealing with. They looked like an incredibly successful employment agency, dealing with professional temps and headhunting missions for companies across the South East. Dane himself gave a smarmy grin from their home page, and I felt an irrational surge of antipathy towards the man. He was way too good-looking, and he knew it. I wondered if the neatly trimmed goatee and stylish suit meant he was gay or merely metrosexual. Of course, I had to admit most straight men were better groomed than I was at that time, new haircut or not.

When James had finished his rundown, he gave me an awkward smile. "I know it's a lot to ask of you, but you'd say if it was more than you could cope with, wouldn't you?"

"Of course. I'll be fine," I said breezily, knowing full well I'd have more than a few late nights working on this account.

"Great. Well, I'll email over the file and let you get on with things, then. Bye for now."

"Bye, James."

I kept the fixed grin in place until I'd switched off the

webcam, then slumped back into the chair. Moments like these, I knew I was kidding myself when I said it was only the dialysis regime that kept me out of the workplace. If a twenty-minute conversation completely wiped me out, how on earth would I cope with a day in the office?

Still, no point in fretting about things that couldn't be changed. I pinched the bridge of my nose, thought productive thoughts, and set about my latest assignment.

Of course, forty minutes into my supposed work binge, I found myself navigating to my favourite adult DVD site—the one I knew used Ollie's company for deliveries. I tried searching for "parcel delivery guy", came up with nothing and eventually struck on using "mailman" as the search term. I added a couple of the most promising-looking titles to my basket and selected the guaranteed next day delivery option. Then I felt a bit guilty and went browsing for X-Men comics. At least that way I'd have something I could talk about next time Ollie knocked on the door to deliver my porn. It's not like I could tell him I had a recently discovered kink for parcel delivery guys, could I?

# Chapter Three

The next morning, I stood naked in front of my wardrobe, willing it to give me a break. Ollie would be here at some point in the next few hours, if the online parcel tracking information was correct, and I wanted to be wearing something at least marginally more stylish than I had last time. I glared at the row of suits I could no longer fit into before reassuring myself that Ollie probably wouldn't be into that look anyway as he had that whole skate-punk thing going on. Assuming he was even into guys, which he probably wasn't. And even if he was, why on earth would he be interested in me?

I had to keep telling myself that because I was starting to act like Zoe used to when she complained about having *nothing to wear,* despite her wardrobe bursting at the seams. I stretched up to the top shelf where I'd stowed all my clubbing gear, and as I did, the tape holding my catheter tube in place pulled free. I looked down to see it swinging loose and wondered who I thought I was kidding. There was no way I'd be able to disguise the outline of it through the close-fitting T-shirts, and then there was the fluid-filled belly of doom to take into account too. I had thought about skipping a bag and staying up late to fit it in before sleep, but it wasn't like I could rely on Ollie coming at all—the tracking had been wrong before—and I figured I should probably put my health first.

Doctor Singh would be so proud of me.

I fingered the fabric of one of my favourite shirts and sighed. I knew I should probably just get rid of them all, but there was still a chance of getting some kind of life back before I got too old to wear it again. I just had to wait for someone with the right blood group and tissue type to die in a horrible accident that left a kidney intact. And their pancreas too, so I could be cured of the diabetes at the same time. God, while I was at it, why not wish for them to leave me a fortune as well? I felt like a complete and utter bastard wishing death on a random stranger just so that I could go out on the pull, so I shut the door on temptation and went to the chest of drawers where I stored all my day-to-day clothes. My stretchy, elasticated, baggy clothes. Great.

I found a Wolverine T-shirt in vibrant blue and pulled that on, along with the least dorky-looking pair of trackie bottoms. It would have to do. At least I didn't have a mullet anymore.

The doorbell chimed.

"Hang on a minute!" I called. I looked around for the tape I used to hold the tube down but couldn't see it anywhere. Must have knocked it down the back of the bed again. Good thing the T-shirt was so roomy, as it hid the bloating as well as disguising the outline of the untethered catheter tube.

God, I was attractive these days.

I almost tripped over my own feet getting to the front door, then froze when I saw the purple-haired form outside. I had to bully my legs into getting going again. It was what I'd been hoping for, wasn't it? Only thing was, I was paranoid all those fantasies I'd been indulging in—the ones about Ollie taking one look at the new haircut then pushing his way in and tearing all my clothes off—would show on my face. I ran my hands over my belly to remind myself of the real situation. Fantasy Ben didn't look like this. Fantasy Ben had a nice set of abs and boundless energy. Yeah, fantasy Ben could go fuck himself, the smug git.

"Hey there," Ollie said when I opened the door, that million-watt grin lighting up his face again. "Like the hair. Got another one of these for you."

"Thanks." I tried to kick-start my mouth into saying something interesting, but it refused to cooperate and decided it wanted to dry out instead. I suppose it was slightly less embarrassing than drooling over him. In an effort not to stare, I forced my gaze away and fixed it on the front garden next door. There was only a low, brick wall separating my spartan, gravel driveway with Mrs. Felpersham's garden, but it was like another world over there. She'd crammed it full of blowsy pink flowers, a wooden wishing well and more garden gnomes than you could shake a stick at. Those gnomes always gave me the heebie-jeebies, but at least there were plenty to keep my eyes occupied at times like this.

"Oh, sweet! I've got that exact same T-shirt! 'Course, mine's a bit smaller." Ollie started bouncing up and down on his heels, and I wanted to lick him all over, he looked so appealing. At that thought, despite being full of dialysate, I felt my cock starting to stir. It's a good thing I was in the XXX-Large version of the Wolverine shirt. Still, I leant forward a little just to make sure nothing showed.

My mind got stuck on the idea of how much I wanted to see him in that T-shirt and then out of it. I started to worry that I was going to blurt it out by accident, so I kept my mouth firmly shut. I must have looked like a right stuck-up twat. Didn't seem to bother Ollie, though.

"I should bring some of those comics round for you to read. It would be good to have someone to chat about them with. Most of my other friends think I'm nuts, you know?"

What? *Other* friends? Did that mean he considered me a friend? We'd only known each other for a few weeks. I realised I needed to speak, and fast, if I wasn't to make a terrible impression and get struck off that friends list.

"Yeah, uh, great. I mean, I'd like that, if you don't mind lending your stuff to a stranger." Great. Now I'd called myself a stranger when he was trying to be friendly.

"Nah, it's cool. I know where you live, after all." He gave me another huge grin that made his cheeks dimple. It really wasn't fair. No one should be allowed to be that cute.

We did the parcel-signing thing, and I instructed my hands to stay where they were and not go straying over to stroke his. He had a graze on the knuckles of his left hand, and I wanted to kiss it better, like I used to with Zoe.

"Looks nasty," I said.

"Oh yeah," Ollie said, flexing his hand. "Skating injury. I was going for a 360 kickflip, but I bollocksed it up. Looks worse than it felt."

Shit, I must have been staring. I hoped I hadn't started making kissy lips or anything.

"I didn't know you were a skateboarder," I said. After all, dressing like a skater was no guarantee of actually taking part in it. "Are you any good?"

He twisted his lips in a half smile and wrinkled his nose, but his eyes still sparkled. "Not as good as I'd like, but that's okay. I know I'm never gonna compete, or anything, but it's fun. I like hanging out with the guys, you know? Studying their technique."

There was this glint to his eyes, and I thought maybe he was trying to imply something, but I wasn't going to risk making a fool of myself and spooking a straight bloke.

I mumbled something even I couldn't understand and hugged my parcel close. Then I worried that it would pull my T-shirt in tight and reveal the tube, so I dropped my arms to my sides and tried to look casual.

"What have you got today?" Ollie asked, pointing at the parcel. "Another film? You should sign up for that Love Film thingy, you know? Save you a heap of money."

"Uh, no... I mean, they're not all films." Shit, why hadn't I prepared a lie for if he asked me that? I was rubbish at making things up on the spot, and I wasn't about to tell him it was a couple of DVDs about delivery guys who liked to deliver more than just the mail to their eager customers. "This is work stuff," I added lamely.

"Oh yeah? What is it you do?"

Okay, this I could handle. The trick was trying to make it sound interesting enough so as not to send other people into a coma. "Software design. I'm currently working on the code for a complex payroll system."

Ollie nodded, and I was pleased to see that his eyes hadn't glazed over. "So does that make you your own boss? Nice one."

"Not exactly, but I only have to check in with him now and again. I'm mostly left to my own devices."

"Ah, that's not so bad, then. I wanna be my own boss one day. I've got two bosses, and they're both bastards, but at least the one in the café lets me have free coffee on my shifts."

"You work in a café too? How on earth do you fit that in?" And how the hell did he have the energy to get up in the morning after holding down two jobs? "You must be knackered."

"Nah, it's no trouble. I just do a couple of hours there early evenings and on weekends. Need to save up some money coz I want to open a little café by the ramps in Caversham Park. I could sell proper coffee and watch the guys skate all day, and whenever it gets quiet, I could draw. That'd be well sweet." He had this faraway look in his eyes that made him look so young and innocent. He had to be at least eighteen, though, right? It's not like they'd let someone who'd just passed their driving test out in a big van like that.

Then the sparkle was back. "Shit, man, I'd better get going or someone's gonna wonder where I am. Listen, I'll bring those comics next time, all right?"

"Yeah, great. I mean, that would be really kind of you."

"No trouble." He grinned, and for a moment, I thought he was about to hug me or something, but then the moment was gone, and he was bouncing down the drive.

"Bye, Ollie." God, I envied that energy. And I was so fucking desperate to get my hands on those pert buttocks and squeeze.

"Laters," he threw over his shoulder with a smirk, and I flushed as I realised I'd been caught in the act again. Damn it! It was such a tease, trying to work out just what his arse looked like under those baggy trousers.

That night, I watched both the DVDs, but my mind wasn't really on the overly groomed actors grunting away on-screen. I was picturing a shock of purple hair bobbing between my legs, those big brown eyes giving me that sparkle as he sucked me down. I came harder than I had in a long time.

As I lay in bed in a post-orgasmic haze, I knew I needed to do something about this growing obsession. The question was, what? It was a Friday, and I didn't have anything else on order, so I wouldn't see him again until at least Tuesday. Three whole days without so much of a glimpse of purple hair. It was going to be torture, but it wasn't like I knew where to find him outside of work...or did I?

The following afternoon, I pulled up outside one of the tall, terraced houses lining Caversham Park and killed the engine before hunkering down in my seat and turning to stare at the skate ramps through the railings.

It was at times like these I wished I had a less conspicuous car. Okay, Ollie had never seen it as it was kept locked in the garage, but a vintage red MG convertible has a way of getting you noticed. I'd bought it as soon as Zoe moved out of home, in the period I was starting to think of as my midlife crisis, even though I'd only been in my late twenties. I'd spent a couple of heady years of making up for all the normal, adolescent things I'd missed out on while bringing up Zoe, but with the added advantage of me having enough money to shower around to ensure I always got plenty of dick. And okay, I know I took it too far with the recklessness and the drugs and the casual sex, but I was paying for it now, wasn't I?

The April afternoon sun was low in the sky, and it only lit the skater on the ramps when he was at the top, but I could tell that it wasn't Ollie even from this distance. There were a few other figures in the gloom at the base of the ramps, but it was too murky to distinguish them from each other.

What the hell was I doing here? It was no use trying to pretend to myself that I'd just stopped by while in the neighbourhood, because I'd taken a ten-minute detour through Reading traffic to swing by here on my way back from Zoe's place. No, I had in fact hit a new low: predatory older man stalking nubile twink at the bloody playground. I was a fucking chickenhawk.

I groaned and sank lower in my seat. I just needed some human contact. Some intimate, male human contact. Maybe I should just go ahead and do what Zoe kept suggesting—sign up with gaydar.co.uk and be honest about my situation. There must be a few blokes out there who wouldn't care about the catheter tube so long as they got a decent seeing to. Trouble was, I wasn't even confident I could promise that anymore. I'd probably be so nervous about my weakened body I wouldn't be able to get it up, let alone give their arse a proper pounding.

And more to the point, I didn't want just anyone. I didn't want simply a convenient hole to stick my dick into. I wanted Ollie with his gappy-tooth grin, boundless energy and sinfully delicious arse.

I had to stop thinking about his arse. There would only be one thing worse than spying on teenage boys in the park, and that was doing so with a stiffy.

I was just about to start the engine and take myself back home when a familiar voice stayed my hand. Ollie!

"And besides, it's not like you're using it right now."

"I said no! Fucking hell, Oll."

The other voice was gruffer, deeper than Ollie's, with just a trace of a Pakistani accent. I scanned the street and saw the two figures crossing the road some fifteen yards ahead. They turned in my direction, and I froze. Would they notice me more or less if I sat still? Could I pretend to be visiting someone in the nearby houses if Ollie spotted me? Just how good a liar was I, anyway?

Whatever the argument had been about, Ollie seemed to have let it go, because when he next spoke, I could hear his smile lighting up the words.

"What do you want for dinner tonight? I was thinking I could make pie and mash, seeing as how it's your favourite."

Jealousy burst through me with a stinging pain.

"There's no point trying to get around me like that, and I'm not accepting sexual favours either," the other lad answered.

I gripped the wheel so tight I'd leave permanent dents in the leather.

The two of them walked straight past the car, and I was treated to a vision of Ollie in baggy jeans and a skinny-fit T-shirt with what looked like rhinestone writing on the front. I wasn't able to decipher it because I was too busy getting a look at my rival: a tall, dark-skinned guy with a shaved head that gleamed even in the dusk. Shit, they looked good together. Better than Ollie and I ever would.

"You're no fun," Ollie grumbled. "Not even a blowjob?"

"Not a chance."

"I'll just ask your wife, then, shall I?" Ollie suggested, punching the tall guy on the arm. "I know she's the one who wears the trousers in your relationship, anyway."

As Ollie's friend laughed and scuffled with him, relief flooded through me, turning my arms to jelly. They slithered down the steering wheel and landed on my lap. I sat there until the sound of their banter had faded into the distance, then drove home as fast as I dared.

# Chapter Four

After my spying mission at the ramps, I tried to go cold turkey for a few days and didn't order any more DVDs. Of course, I'd forgotten about the one that was out of stock when I'd ordered it, and consequently, I really wasn't expecting Ollie to be at the door on Monday morning.

What I'd been expecting was Mrs. Felpersham, the old biddy who lives in the gnome-infested house next door and who insists on calling round once a week to ask how I'm doing. I wouldn't mind if it were purely an innocent enquiry, but I swear she's just looking for a chance to snoop around my flat and pass judgment. I once made the mistake of inviting her in for a cup of tea after Zoe and I first moved in, but after hearing her lecture me about leaving the television on and how it would rot Zoe's innocent brain, I decided not to let her get past the front door again.

So that's why I was still bleary-eyed and in my dressing gown when I opened the front door.

"Oh shit!" I exclaimed, then desperately tried to backpedal as I saw Ollie's face fall. "I mean, I'd have got dressed if I'd known you were coming. I thought it was my neighbour. Her, next door." I pointed at Mrs. Felpersham's front door, which sat directly opposite mine over the driveway. I could've sworn the net curtain on the window next to it twitched.

Ollie gave me a lopsided grin. "I see. And do you normally answer the door to her in your PJs...or whatever it is you're wearing under there?" His gaze panned downwards, and I was acutely aware that I was in nothing more than a pair of boxers under the towelling robe. "Should I be jealous she's getting special treatment?"

Was he flirting with me? I wished I could just come out with it. Ask him what his intentions towards me were, like one of the heroines in those boring BBC period dramas Zoe used to make me watch with her. I was plucking up my courage to speak when Ollie got there first.

"Hey, nice slippers."

There's only one thing more humiliating than the man you have a desperate crush on catching you answering the door in your dressing gown, and that's when he catches you wearing the bright green monster feet slippers your little sister gave you for Christmas. Especially when your pasty white and hairy shins are visible below the hem of your dressing gown.

I mumbled something about not having bought them myself, but whether or not he believed me, I had no idea. I was signing for the parcel and trying to work out how I was going to phrase my "so, are you gay or what?" query, when the door opposite finally swung open.

"Young man, where's my parcel? It was meant to come last week."

"I'll warn you now," I muttered so Mrs. F. wouldn't be able to hear, "she won't take no for an answer."

Ollie rolled his eyes and turned to face her over the wall. "I'm sorry, I don't have any record of a delivery to your address. Are you sure it wasn't coming by a different carrier?"

Mrs. F. screwed up her nose and peered at him. "Don't try and tell me I don't know what I'm talking about, young man. I'll have you know I ordered my little gnome last Monday, and they always come by the end of the week in a bright yellow van."

I groaned both at the idea of yet another gnome polluting her front garden with its creepy good cheer, and at what poor Ollie was about to endure before he managed to get away.

"Sorry, mate," Ollie said on his way down the driveway, "but that's really not my problem. You'll have to get in touch with whoever you ordered it from." He turned to fix me with that grin I dreamt about every night. I was willing to swear there was more than just friendly interest there. "Catch you later, yeah?"

"Well, really!" Mrs. F. protested as Ollie's van peeled off down the road. "What a thoroughly insolent young man. I've a good mind to report him to his boss."

"Yeah, why don't you do that? And while you're at it, you can check if you've got your facts straight for a change."

I slammed my front door on her shocked expression. Bloody interfering old baggage. I'd been so close to asking him that time.

I'd just have to order some more porn.

I was having one of my between bag "recreational breaks" the next morning when I heard Zoe's key in the door. I hit the pause button, turned off the TV and crossed my fingers, hoping Zoe hadn't heard the rhythmic grunting coming from the speakers. Fortunately, another baggy T-shirt hid my rapidly subsiding erection, but I still took a moment to think unsexy thoughts before getting up from the sofa.

"I swear, those gnomes next door are breeding. It's a bloody infestation. You should call Rentokil."

Yep, reminding me of the eerie garden next door where a

thousand ceramic eyes peered out at unsuspecting passersby was an excellent way to deal with inappropriate arousal. I'd have to remember that next time I saw Ollie and his delicious, tempting backside.

The doorbell rang. It couldn't be. There's no way the disc I'd ordered yesterday would be here in time for today. But I peered out of the window, and there was Ollie's van parked outside.

"I'll get it," Zoe trilled and was off before I had a chance to protest.

I raced after her as fast as I could, which was more of a slow lumber, and reached the door just as she was telling Ollie how she'd heard all about him.

"Thanks, sis, I'll take it from here." I hauled Zoe out of the way and turned so that Ollie wouldn't be able to see me glaring a warning at her. Zoe just stuck her tongue out at me and slunk off, no doubt to listen in from behind the kitchen door.

"Sorry about that. You know family. Always out to embarrass you."

Ollie gave an odd smile that twisted his mouth out of shape, and I could have kicked myself. Who knew what his relationship with his family was like, assuming he even had any? Should I ask him? I was trying to work out how to phrase an innocent enquiry about them when he broke the silence.

"Just dropping these off for you. I've got all my faves here." He held out a Forbidden Planet plastic bag stuffed full of comics.

"Thanks. You didn't have to do this."

"Nah, it's fine. Actually, you're doing me a bit of a favour. I'm staying at a mate's house at the moment, but his missus wants my stuff out of there before she has the baby."

I took a moment to digest this information. Did Ollie mean

he was about to be made homeless by the tall Asian bloke's wife? Could I offer him a place to stay without creeping him out? I didn't dare ask. Not yet. I barely knew him, after all. I turned my attention back to the comics.

"These look like they've been well loved," I observed, lifting out a dog-eared graphic novel. Most of the guys I'd known who were into comics were so anal about them it was unreal.

"Yeah, I know they're not in those silly little Mylar bags, but I'd rather enjoy them than get all wound up about their resale value, you know?"

"I'll look after them for you."

"That's cool; I know you will. You seem like the cautious type." I wasn't sure if he was mocking me or not.

"I can be spontaneous."

Ollie quirked his eyebrows. "Oh yeah? Prove it."

He held my gaze steadily, and my stomach flipped over as my body broke out in a sweat. Shit. It would have been so easy to lean forward and kiss his smiling lips, but I just couldn't. Especially not with Zoe inside somewhere and probably spying, if I knew her. Besides which, who's to say that would be welcome? Just because he was friendly and a bit alternative, didn't mean he was into guys.

"Look," Ollie said eventually, fiddling with the leather bracelets round one of his skinny wrists, "I should probably be going. If you want to read the comics, that's cool. If not, I can take them back. No trouble."

"No, uh, I mean, yeah, I want to read them. Could do with a distraction. How about you call by next time you're passing, and I'll give them back."

"Yeah, I'll do that, and you can let me know which is your favourite. Laters, Ben," he called, already bouncing down the driveway.

"I told you so," Zoe said, her arms wrapping around me from behind. "Definitely interested."

I turned and indicated my belly, but she just gave me a blank look. I huffed. "I'm all ill and bloated. He's not going to want to do anything about it even if he does like me."

"Rubbish. You don't look half as bad as you think you do, Benj. You might be a bit flabbier than you used to be, but you're not overweight." Zoe reached out and pulled my T-shirt tight against my belly before I managed to squirm away. "All that's happened is you've filled out a bit, like all blokes do when they hit their thirties. How about I take you shopping this weekend? I reckon you'd look pretty hot with some decent clothes that fit you properly. You'll be able to go out and pull someone your own age then."

"I've got a tube sticking out of my belly!"

"Yeah? So what? You seem to be the only one who gives a shit about that. You going to let it ruin the rest of your life by hiding away with your dirty DVDs, or are you going to man up, take a few risks and get on with living?" She glared at me with her hands on her hips. Jesus, if she only knew how much she looked like Mum just then.

I leant down to pick up the bag of comics. "I'm not allowed to take risks anymore, you know that. Now if you've finished your little lecture, I want to go and have a look at these."

I tried to make as dignified a retreat as possible, but the bag was heavy, and I swayed, stumbling into the wall. Before I knew what had happened, Zoe was there, hooking my arm around her shoulders and helping me to my bedroom.

"You should have a lie-down. Chill for a bit."

"Maybe I'll just rest my eyes for a minute." I sank back into my pillows, sleep claiming me almost instantly.

# Chapter Five

Zoe worked in the restaurant all day Saturday, so we didn't get to go shopping until Sunday. It'd been a couple of years since I'd walked around the pedestrianised centre of Reading, but aside from an awful lot more mobile phone shops than I remembered, nothing much seemed to have changed. The April sunshine lit up the same grand old buildings and gilded the same crowds meandering around and spilling out onto the pavements outside coffee shops and bars.

It was me who was different.

Every step seemed to take an enormous effort. Zoe kept tugging on my arm, as if she was desperate to get to whichever store was going to make a dent in my bank balance next. I suppose we were working to a bit of a tight schedule, as I needed to be back home by two o'clock to drain my belly.

As we passed Marks and Sparks, I peered down the road, hoping for a glimpse of the bar I used to frequent with the guys from work. It hadn't been a particularly gay-friendly place—although I got a definite vibe off one of the bartenders—but it had been great for picking up a gram of coke before heading somewhere a shade pinker. Nostalgia welled up inside me. Not for the drugs and the mindless hookups that followed, but for the sense of opportunity and hope those evenings always began with.

"Come on, Benj. I want to check out what they've got in Gap. There were these really smart gilets in the window a few weeks ago, and I reckon you'd rock that look."

"Gilets? What the hell's a gilet?"

Zoe rolled her eyes. "Gawd, and there was me thinking gay blokes were meant to know all about fashion. Whatever would Gok Wan make of you?"

"Dunno, but I doubt even he'd be willing to tell me I look good naked."

"Could we lose the self-pity for a while, please? There's nothing wrong with the way you look. You've got a nice face, and you're tall with broad shoulders. Case closed."

Since I didn't want to go into the way the catheter tube stuck out of me like an alien growth, or the bald patch I had to keep shaving on my belly so I could stick the tube down, I wisely decided to change the subject. I was probably far too obsessed with my lower abdomen, but as it was so close to my favourite part of my anatomy, could I be blamed?

"Zo, I know you're used to spending all day on your feet, but I need a rest. I'm all shopped out, and these bags are heavy." They really were as well. I had three large bags on each arm, all stuffed full of clothing that Zoe assured me I simply *had* to buy.

She looked like she was about to protest, but then something melted, and she gave a wry smile. "Sorry. You do look a bit pale. Okay, how about here? Unless you'd rather find a Starbucks or a Nero?"

Here was a rather homespun, ramshackle-looking place that I'd probably not have looked twice at back in the day, but right then, I was so exhausted I'd have been willing to stop at a bloody MacDonald's.

As the outdoor tables were all packed full of smokers and

those desperate to banish their winter pallor with the spring sunshine, we headed inside. I collapsed into a chair at the nearest free table I could find while Zoe stacked the bags onto a spare chair for me.

She glanced around. "Looks like it's waiter service. If someone takes our order while I'm on the bog, could you get me a decaf skinny latte with a shot of hazelnut?" She left for the toilets before I had a chance to protest at being left to order the most girly drink possible, short of one with cocktail umbrellas and plastic parrots in it.

I was staring at the menu, trying to decide whether a fruit smoothie would take me over my potassium allowance for the day, when a familiar voice sent a charge of electricity right through me.

"Hey, Ben, good to see you, mate."

I wrenched my head around so fast I was in serious danger of whiplash. Ollie looked different to how he usually did, and it wasn't just the lack of forest-green polyester. I was used to looking down on him from standing, but from this angle, his face seemed somehow stronger, more confident. The Manga-kitten effect of those big brown eyes was lessened, and his jaw jutted out more. I flicked my gaze over him quickly, hoping he wouldn't notice. He had on baggy jeans and a skinny-fit black T-shirt under a snug black apron. In case I'd been in any doubt as to his reason for being here, he had an order pad and pen in his hand.

Ollie cleared his throat, and I realised I was well overdue making my reply.

"Hi. Er, nice place you've got here." It wasn't. The table was still sticky from the last occupants, and the decor looked like something Mrs. F. would approve of: all cutesy knickknacks and dried flowers.

Ollie shrugged. “It’s not bad, but the manager never listens to my ideas for improving things. Still, the coffee’s great. Can I get you one? On the house.”

My heart fell. “I’d love to, but I can’t drink coffee. Doctor’s orders.”

“Bummer.” Ollie sounded genuinely upset on my behalf.

“Yeah. It is.” I brandished the menu. “How about a smoothie? Are they any good?”

A wicked grin lit up Ollie’s face. “I could do you one of my specials, if you like. They’ve got a bit more kick than the regular.”

“Kick?”

“I do an awesome dark chocolate, cherry and cranberry smoothie. Well, it’s kind of a milkshake with all the ice-cream that goes in there, but it tastes divine.”

“I bet.” I’d been watching Ollie’s lips as he spoke, imagining just how heavenly they would taste.

“I’ll put you down for one of those, then.”

Shit. “No. Er, better not. Just plain fruit please.”

“It’s not as fattening as you think. Debs, she’s on Weightwatchers, and she still has one every day. Mind you, she starves herself the rest of the time, or so she says.”

I’d have to explain. Better he knew the truth than thought I was someone with an eating disorder.

“I...I can’t. I’m not well right now. I had kidney failure a couple of years ago, and I’m on dialysis now. It really puts a crimp on my lifestyle. I can’t eat anything much, can’t drink alcohol or coffee; I feel like death warmed up. I’ve got to do everything by the book so I don’t end up killing myself. Sorry.” I croaked the last word out.

“Shit, man. That’s rough.” Ollie rubbed the back of his neck and looked awkward. “Don’t know if I could cope without coffee and chocolate.”

Now he was going to do that whole sympathy thing and go on about how sorry he was and how his second-uncle-once-removed had kidney troubles, or some such pointless anecdote about an old codger that would make me feel ancient. I might have the odd grey hair coming through, but I wasn’t ready to join up with the stair lift brigade just yet.

As it was, his next question threw me.

“So, does that mean you’re a cyborg?”

“You what?” I just stared at him, amazed to see the start of that quirky grin at the corners of his mouth.

“You know, like, you’re hooked up to machines in order to stay alive. That makes you a cyborg, technically.”

“Uh, well, I’m not really hooked up to machines.” His face fell for some bizarre reason I couldn’t fathom. I wanted to get the grin back again. “I did that for a while, but I’m on a different form of dialysis now. It’s called Continuous Ambulatory Peritoneal Dialysis.” He looked impressed, so I continued, despite it being the one part of my life I really didn’t want to talk about. “I have to fill my abdomen up with fluid four times a day, then drain it out a few hours later. It’s not all that high-tech or anything. Just a drip stand and a catheter tube going into my belly.”

“You’ve got a tube in your belly? Wow, that’s cool! Can I have a look?”

“No!” I squeaked in alarm.

Ollie pouted momentarily, then looked contrite. “Sorry. Guess I should mind my own business.” He started to back away, and I kicked myself for being a twat.

“No, wait. It’s not that. I’m just a bit... Well, it’s pretty ugly."

"Yeah? Bet I've seen worse. Used to go out with someone who had their navel pierced. Was always getting infected and shit. Looked bloody awful, but I didn't mind getting up close." He stuck his chin out defiantly.

I just stared again, trying to work out if the pronoun avoidance meant he'd just outed himself to me. He'd need to be a bit more obvious for me to be sure. Wearing a rainbow badge with "I'm gay" emblazoned on it would be a help.

"Ollie, a little help, please!"

Ollie jumped at the strident voice coming from the woman behind the counter. "God, I'd better get back. Anything else you wanted?"

I ordered Zoe's pretend coffee and earned a raised eyebrow, but Ollie refrained from commenting.

"Ooh, have I still got time to order something to eat?" Zoe said as she slid back into her chair. "What would you recommend?"

"The sticky toffee cake is to die for. I mean, seriously scrummy."

"Sounds great."

I resolutely refused to watch Ollie as he walked away, aware of Zoe scrutinising me.

"That's your delivery boy, isn't it? The one you fancy."

I blushed, which seemed to be answer enough for her.

"Cute but way too young for you," was her eventual verdict.

"And probably straight too."

Zoe snorted. "Yeah right. Because straight guys are always describing cake as 'scrummy'. He's well into you, it's bloody obvious. Your gaydar's completely screwed, you know that?"

"I don't think anyone ever bothered to issue me with one." I wasn't about to argue with her. Not about the gaydar, anyway.

Ollie was polite but a little more distant when he brought the drinks. Whether that was down to Zoe's presence or that of the large woman with the stern demeanour now manning the counter, I couldn't tell.

I wanted to go and say goodbye when we left, but he was in the middle of making a coffee and the café was too busy. I settled for waving when he looked up and was treated to a grin that jolted through me like I'd just downed a triple espresso.

The next morning found me in new chinos and a black cashmere polo-neck that even I had to admit wasn't too shabby. I hadn't been too sure about the gilet to begin with—it turned out to be nothing more than a glorified bodywarmer—but as the bulk of it effectively covered any hint of the tube, I was a convert.

I was nervous about Ollie seeing me in the new clothes, though. I'd been so worked up about it, I'd had no appetite that morning and had skipped breakfast. It was no wonder I was feeling a bit odd. Like the world was slipping sideways. I'd have to go and have a snack as soon as he'd left—get my blood-sugar level up.

When the doorbell rang, I still had that nervous flutter in my belly, although this time there was a frisson of something else. Was it hope? Confidence? Whatever it was, it felt weird.

"Hey, like the outfit. Are you off out somewhere?"

Shit. Had I overdone it? Zoe had assured me chinos were fine for casual wear. "No, just trying out some of the new threads I bought yesterday."

I looked up from my trousers and plastered a smile on my face, which lasted until Ollie held up my parcel. There was a big tear at one end. It looked like it had been hacked open with a breadknife.

"Sorry about this. It got a bit...damaged in transit. The DVD fell out."

I grabbed it from him, peered into the cardboard packet and groaned. *The Visitor*, a gay porn sci-fi epic starring Logan McCree. It would have to be that one, wouldn't it? I could feel my whole body break out in a sweat.

I couldn't meet Ollie's gaze, so I kept my eyes lowered. That was when I noticed the packing knife hanging off his belt. It was one of those safety ones with the little hooked blade for cutting through tape. The ones that are bloody useless at getting through cardboard neatly.

"Have you been opening my stuff?" Rage tore through me. My hands started to shake. "That's private!"

He just shrugged and gave me a cheeky grin. "Yeah, well, I had to find out what you're into, since you give so little away. You seen it yet? It's a great film—got a proper plot and everything. My ex had it, so I've seen it loads of times. Logan McCree's so fucking hot. Get a load of those tats." He leered, and jealousy washed over me.

Just perfect—he was definitely gay, but now I had to compete with guys like Logan tattooed-dick McCree for his attention. I didn't stop to ask myself when I'd decided I was actually in with a chance, because my blood was roaring in my ears, and things were starting to look funny. Must be the red mist coming down, making things split apart and refuse to glue back together. I now had two purple-haired delivery boys standing on my doorstep.

"Don't know what you're talking about. What's that

sound?" I wasn't sure which of the two Ollies to look at, so I focused somewhere in the middle. "It's like a waterfall."

"Are you all right?" the Ollies asked, their voice distant like they were standing at the other end of a tunnel.

The cheek of it! "Of course I'm all right! Never better." I tried to close the door, but it slipped away from me, and I slid down to the floor. The DVD tumbled out of my hand. I wondered if I'd be able to watch it by running my fingers over the disc.

"Ben? Ben, what's wrong?" There was a loud voice that sounded like it was coming from inside my skull. "Ben? I think you need some help. Maybe a doctor. Shit!"

# Chapter Six

Ollie knelt down beside me, his face up really close. There was only one of him now. I leant forward to kiss him. Slippery boy, dodging me. Huh! Thought he was meant to be gay.

“What are you doing, Ben? I’m not gonna snog you now. You’re ill.”

“I’m always fucking ill,” I told him, but the words sounded slurred and melty. “You should kiss me better.” I pursed up my lips and closed my eyes.

“What do you need? You’d better tell me, or I’m phoning for an ambulance.”

My brain didn’t seem to want to work, so I pointed at the chain around my neck. Ollie frowned but then pulled the Medic alert pendant out from under my gilet. I heard footsteps disappearing down my hall, and the next thing I was aware of was a sickly drink pouring into my mouth and down my chin.

When the world started to make sense again, a wave of breathtaking shame crashed over me. Not only had I neglected myself enough to have an attack—which hadn’t happened for ages—but I’d thrown myself at Ollie. I leant back against the wall and tried to regain my cool. It seemed to have deserted me, and I couldn’t blame it.

“You okay now?” he asked me.

I nodded. I still didn't trust myself not to say something stupid.

"Shit, Ben, you had me worried there. Do you need me to call someone for you?"

"No, it's fine. Just had a hypo. Nothing to worry about. Zoe will be here soon. She'll sort me out."

"Zoe? That's your sister, right?"

"Yeah. She calls in every day on her way into work."

He nodded, but he still didn't look happy. I missed his smile.

"Thanks," I said. "You did exactly the right thing. Sorry I acted like a total wanker. I don't know what I'm doing when I have an attack."

There was that curve of his lips I loved so much. "I thought you were drunk at first," Ollie said.

"No chance." I smiled back. "No alcohol, no coffee, no cigarettes, no sugar, no sex—"

"No sex? What, your doctor told you that?"

I avoided his eyes. "Not really up to going out and pulling, these days," I mumbled.

"But you are allowed to have sex, right?"

Ollie sounded really concerned. I looked up into his espresso-brown eyes and tried to smile as I nodded.

"Well, that's a—"

"Ben! Oh, my God, are you all right?"

Whatever Ollie had been about to say was interrupted by Zoe's arrival.

"I'm fine," I told her, but she wasn't having it.

"You always say that when you're having a hypo." She turned to Ollie. "What's happened? Did you find him like this?"

Ollie took over and explained about his trip to the fridge to find my Lucozade stash, much to my relief as I really didn't feel like being on the receiving end of one of Zoe's "look after yourself" lectures.

It took the two of them to help me to my feet and then get me ensconced on the sofa with my feet up on the coffee table. I noticed Ollie discreetly slip the DVD back into the package and place it on my telly. I should have told him not to bother—Zoe would probably want to borrow the damn thing.

Before he left, Ollie turned to me, looking strangely ill at ease and jiggling on his feet.

"Listen, I'd love to come round this evening and check up on you, but I've got a shift at the café, and I can't really let them down."

Yeah, right. Now he'd seen me properly ill, he couldn't wait to get away. "I don't need a babysitter," I snapped.

"That's not what I meant." Bright spots appeared on Ollie's cheeks. "Christ, you're hard work sometimes."

"Well, there's no need to put yourself out. I'm just a customer, after all." I regretted the words as soon as they were out, but I wasn't going to take them back. He'd seen enough of my weakness for one day.

He shook his head at me, muttering as he left the room. I heard the front door slam.

Zoe came through holding two cups of tea and one of my carefully rationed juice bottles.

"Where's he gone?" she asked. "Benji, did you go and say something stupid?"

I tried to hide my face in the cushions. "Thought you didn't like him."

Zoe huffed. "It's not that I don't like him. He's just a bit young for you. At least he can keep his head in a crisis, though. Would have thought you'd be glad to have him stay for tea."

"He had to get back to work," I mumbled.

She gave me a long look but obviously decided it wasn't worth pursuing that line of questioning when I was due a lecture about looking after myself. I strapped myself in for the ride. Zoe was right, and I knew it.

I had a terrible night. Zoe's words kept echoing round my head, and I cringed with shame every time I recalled how I'd spoken to Ollie. Poor guy must be totally confused about me and my mixed messages. Wouldn't blame him if he didn't want to be friends anymore. I still couldn't swallow Zoe's assertion that he was "well into me", but I certainly didn't want to lose the first real friend I'd made in the last couple of years. I wasn't counting the ones I'd made online, as I'd told them so much bullshit, they had no idea who I really was.

I needed to make amends in some way. I'd have to invite him round, make him coffee or something. He loved coffee, didn't he? And at least I'd get the vicarious pleasure of smelling the stuff even if I couldn't drink any myself. I had a bag of coffee beans in the freezer still, kept just in case Zoe ever needed a pick-me-up on her way into work. My mind made up, I managed a few hours sleep, and although I felt like hell when I eventually woke up, I did manage to pull on some new clothes, eat a bowl of muesli and get my first dialysate bag infused. I was rubbing my eyes in front of my monitor when the doorbell made me jump out of my skin.

I was a bundle of neuroses wrapped up in designer clothing by the time I finally reached the front door. Was he only here because I'd ordered yet another porn DVD? Was he after getting his comics back? How much was I going to have to grovel to get back in his good graces? I knew I couldn't answer any of these questions without opening the door, so I reached out and turned the handle with a sweaty hand.

"Hey, how ya doing?" Ollie asked, a small smile playing around his lips. He started twirling his wristbands and was jiggling more than usual. "Um, I'm sorry about storming off yesterday. I'm not usually such a drama queen, but I was a bit shaken up by the whole thing."

I was flabbergasted. I stared at him with my mouth hanging open until the unease in his eyes made me remember my manners. I pulled the door wide open. "You got time to come in for a moment? I could make you a coffee to say sorry for being such an ungrateful tosser."

He grinned as if in relief, then tore back a Velcro strip on one of his wristbands to reveal a watch face. "Yeah, I could probably spare fifteen minutes or so. I mean, I shouldn't, but who's gonna know? I can just say I got stuck in traffic." He gave me a wicked smile and had a glint in his eyes that made my heart start to pound.

I wordlessly led the way to my kitchen, trying desperately to convince my body that soaking itself in sweat was not the best plan of action right now. Needless to say, it didn't bloody well listen to me.

"Wow! Great place you've got here. I was too panicked to notice it all yesterday." Ollie spun around in the middle of the kitchen, peered out over the courtyard garden, then his gaze skittered over my coffeemaker. "Shit, you've got an Elektra Micro Casa! These things are fucking beautiful." He stroked a hand over the brass body. "Looks proper steampunk, that does. Like I said, you've got great taste."

He turned to me, and my mouth dried up. I swallowed

hard. “You want a coffee, then?”

Ollie shook his head, a mischievous smile quirking his lips. “Not really. Maybe next time, though.”

He took a step closer, his eyes sparkling, and I started to panic at my body’s instinctive reaction to him. I couldn’t get properly hard when I was bloated with fluid, could I? I was starting to doubt my previous certainty.

“Juice?” I offered. “Soda water?” Anything to take my mind off the way my blood was racing south.

“There is something I’d like to taste,” Ollie said, stepping well into my personal space. I took a step back and ended up trapped against the worktop.

“Yeah?” I croaked, unable to take my eyes off his as he moved right up close until we were practically touching. I could feel the heat radiating off him, and I wanted nothing more than to pull him to me, but my hands seemed to be glued to the worktop.

“Yeah,” Ollie replied, then slipped his arms around my waist and craned up on tiptoe until our lips brushed together.

# Chapter Seven

"Hnnugh!" My breath escaped me with an embarrassing protest, but Ollie just smiled and hooked a hand around my neck to pull my head down. This time, I was prepared for him and opened my lips to his probing tongue. He kissed enthusiastically—more energy and desire than technique—but he tasted incredible, like mocha with cream. I took over the kiss, slowing it down so that our teeth wouldn't clash anymore. I sucked on his tongue, and Ollie made this little noise that sounded like he'd gone to heaven. It was the sexiest thing I'd ever heard. Jesus Christ, I needed to keep my hands to myself, or I was going to grab hold of his arse and frot against him until I came in my pants. I pulled back, panting, my forehead resting against his.

Then his hand dropped down and groped me through my jeans.

"You'd better stop that," I protested, but I hadn't even convinced myself, so I wasn't surprised when he ignored me.

"What have we got here, then?" he asked. "Feels like a bit of a monster. Think I'd better take a closer look."

He slid his other hand up inside my T-shirt, and I panicked, twisting away. Too close to the tube. Too close to all that fluid inside me.

He knitted his brow and gave me a stern look. "What are

you scared of, Ben? I know you want this too."

"Just, I'm not attractive anymore. My abs have disappeared. I've got a tube." It sounded lame even to me.

"I don't care about the fucking tube, all right?"

"You say that now, but you haven't seen it." I didn't want to tell him about the bald patches. It would sound so bloody vain.

Ollie gave me a pitying look, then pushed up one of his sleeves. I gasped when I saw his tattoo. It was designed to look like his flesh had been flayed, revealing a biomechanical network of metal cables and machinery underneath. It was beautiful, in the most unsettling way. I ran a finger down the curve of one inked cable.

"You see? I'm into all that shit. You don't have to hide it from me."

Maybe I could trust him. I wanted to, I knew that much. My skin was howling for his touch.

"Well?" he asked. "Can I see you?"

I nodded, sucked in my stomach as much as possible, then lifted my T-shirt. The catheter tube was taped down in a curve under my bellybutton—the position I'd found most comfortable when clothed. Ollie dropped to his knees in front of me and stroked gently along the length of the tube, up to where it disappeared inside me, about two inches above and to the left of my navel. He didn't touch the skin right by the entry site but pressed a kiss to one of my shaved patches, next to the tape. I shuddered, overcome by the sensation of his soft lips against my naked skin.

"Wow, that's amazing," he said. I could feel his warm breath on my skin and my eyes started to prickle.

"It doesn't bother you?" I had to know he wasn't just pretending to make me feel better.

Ollie huffed and rolled his eyes. “Does it look like it bothers me?” He indicated the bulge in his trousers, and I had to admit that no, he didn’t look all that perturbed.

Huh.

I pulled my shirt the rest of the way off and stared down at him. It had been so long. Too long. Nearly two years since a man had touched me like this.

But I really didn’t want to think about that last time.

His hand went to my crotch, and he deftly undid the buttons. I couldn’t speak, couldn’t move, just watched him as he pulled down my jeans and boxers as one. My cock sprang free, so much more eloquent and lively than I was. I couldn’t believe it had managed to get that excited even when I was full of fluid, but quite clearly it couldn’t give a monkey’s about that. Maybe I could learn something from Ollie and my dick if the two of them combined forces. Hold that thought…

Ollie breathed on the head of my cock, pulling back the foreskin and giving me a wet lick that felt so good it made me groan. I had to look down. I had to see what he was doing, even if it did mean I had a view of the tube. Actually, that might be a good thing. It would stop me humiliating myself further by coming as fast as a horny teenager.

Ollie smiled up at me and nuzzled my balls. “Wish I could really take my time over this, but I’d better not spend too long right now. That okay? I can come back this evening and suck you properly. Want you to fuck me too, if that’s what you’re into. You top, right? I mean, I hope you do, coz my arse was made for fucking.”

I nodded, breathless, all my words forgotten in the incendiary rush of lust his offer had kick-started.

He didn’t waste any more time on words—just licked me from root to tip, then opened wide and swallowed me down, his hands clutching my arse to pull me in deeper. I quickly discovered that the frantic passion he'd put into his kisses extended to his blowjob technique, but I wasn't complaining. The heat, the incredible suction, the writhing of his tongue all combined to make my dick feel like it was about to explode. I wanted to hold back, to make it last, but with Ollie staring up at me with those big, molten-chocolate eyes, his lips stretched wide around me as he moaned with pleasure like I was some kind of delicious treat—well, I had to give in to it.

My desire rose and rose, filling me up inside until I could burst. I started rocking a little in rhythm with Ollie. I heard myself grunting. What was that all about? I never normally made much noise when I was wanking. I looked at the tube to ground me, but then I realised that Ollie was looking at it too, his pupils growing wider as he dropped a hand down to his groin, fumbled with his trouser fastenings and took hold of his prick. Was he really going to get off looking at that thing?

But then his gaze met mine again, and nothing else mattered as I froze. I tried to warn him, tried to pull his head away, but it was too late. My balls shot their load while he was still sucking on me, my fingers grasping his hair. I couldn't help it, I grabbed on to those purple locks and thrust in deep, my cock throbbing as bliss thundered through me and escaped in a hoarse cry.

Exhausted, I slumped back and watched him finish. Watched him looking up at me, moaning with pleasure, his hand blurring until he stuttered to a finish, creamy jets of spunk squirting on my legs, my jeans, my kitchen cupboards... Far hotter than any come-shot I'd ever seen on my DVDs. This one was just for me.

"Wow, Ben, that was... Christ, that was fucking amazing." He rose on unsteady feet and collapsed against me, panting hard. I could feel his softening cock press against mine, hot and damp and sexy as hell. He wriggled against me, his stomach rubbing the tube, pressing against all my bloated flesh, but this time, I didn't mind. This time, I pulled him close and used my other hand to tilt his head back so I could kiss his swollen lips.

The taste of my salty jizz in his mocha-sweet mouth made my taste buds dance. It was perfection, even when he got overexcited and our teeth clashed painfully. He pulled away, breathless with laughter.

"I'd better get going," Ollie said, looking at his watch. "Shit! I'm gonna have to drive like a maniac to finish my round on time."

"You'll come back later, though?" I didn't want to sound all needy, but I didn't think I could bear him being away from me for too long. I wanted to stay in this little bubble of ours, where I felt happy and desirable and free from anxiety.

"You try stopping me." Ollie pressed a quick kiss to my lips before tucking himself away and zipping up his trousers. To look at him, you wouldn't know what he'd just been up to. Not unless you'd seen him ten minutes before when his lips were about five shades lighter and nowhere near as swollen.

I, on the other hand, was naked, apart from a pair of spunk-spattered jeans pooled around my ankles. I made a half-hearted attempt to reach for my T-shirt.

He grinned and gave me a little wave on his way out of the kitchen. I was too knackered to move.

"Laters, Ben."

I couldn't wait.

It wasn't until three hours later when I walked into my bedroom and saw the stack of dialysate boxes that the bubble burst. What had I been thinking? The drip stand I could probably hide in the wardrobe, but I had no chance of shifting all those boxes out—they weighed a ton. I sat down heavily on the edge of the bed and started hooking myself up to drain the last bag. Maybe I could borrow the throw from the sofa and chuck it over the boxes. The brick red wouldn't really go with the dove-grey-and-olive colour scheme in the bedroom, though, and it would probably just end up drawing attention to them.

I should have kept Zoe's old room as a spare bedroom rather than turning it into an office. We could have slept in there. Of course, I was making an assumption that he'd actually want to stay the night. How much did I really know about Ollie? I knew his mouth tasted like chocolate and he gave great head, but I knew nothing concrete about his life. I had no idea where he lived or what his last name was. I didn't even know his phone number, for fuck's sake. Maybe he did this sort of thing with other guys he delivered to, like some randy porn cliché. I had no reason to think I was anything special.

Except for the way he'd looked at me when he stroked the skin on my belly.

My mobile rang, and I considered leaving it but then fished it out of my pocket.

"Hello?" I snapped.

"Good afternoon, is that Mr. Ben Lethbridge?" a woman's voice asked.

"You'd better not be trying to sell me something," I growled.

She was ever the professional. "I'm calling from the Oxford Transplant Centre. I have some good news for you, but I'll need to ask you a few security questions first to confirm your identity."

I could hardly hear her through the noise of my whirling thoughts but answered the questions on autopilot.

"Okay, that's all confirmed. Mr. Lethbridge. Are you currently at your home in Reading?"

I answered, although the words sounded choked, and my heart was about to drum its way through my rib cage.

"That's good. I'm going to need to ask you to pack an overnight bag and make your way here straight away. We have a possible match for a kidney and pancreas donor. Please don't eat or drink anything as you'll be going straight into surgery if we have a positive cross-match and your physical examination is clear. Do you have any questions you'd like to ask me?"

My mind raced. I knew there were things I could ask, but I also knew they weren't allowed to tell me any personal details about the donor. In the end, it was simpler just to say no and hang up the phone.

I sat there for a long moment, stunned. Fear and excitement lurked somewhere inside me, but right now, it was hard to get any kind of purchase on my emotions. I'd hoped for this for so long, and now the possibility of a transplant was so close, I just felt numb. In the end, I picked up the phone again and called Zoe.

Her high-pitched squeals made me feel even weirder inside, but at least after talking to her, I was able to get up and pack a bag while I waited for her VW Beetle to pull up outside. I wondered about what reading matter to take with me. I was currently stuck in the middle of a heavy-going sci-fi series that wasn't really gripping me. My gaze fell on the pile of comics, and my heart gave a pang. Shit, how was I going to let Ollie know what was going on? I scribbled a quick explanation for my absence on a piece of printer paper, added my mobile number, then wondered where to leave it. I wasn't willing to pin it on the front door as an open invitation for any passing burglars to break in and help themselves.

I looked over my driveway at Mrs. F.'s front door. She was always there, wasn't she? Moments later, I was at her door, explaining about the possible donor match. Her face softened.

"That's wonderful news, Benjamin. I do hope it works out for you."

I thanked her, then took a deep breath. "Would you mind handing this to my friend when he calls by later? You remember the delivery driver from the other day? The one you thought was rude?"

Mrs. F. frowned but took the letter. "How could I forget with hair like that? Now, Benjamin, are you sure you know what you're doing, befriending young men of his persuasion and letting them into your home?"

I couldn't believe my ears. "His *persuasion*?"

"You know what I mean." She lowered her voice and leaned forwards. "Homosexuals."

How could she have picked up on Ollie, but not on me after all these years? I shook my head, glad I wasn't the only one with faulty gaydar. "Mrs. Felpersham, I'll choose my friends however I see fit, and I'm especially happy to have homosexual friends because I'm gay myself."

Mrs. F.'s eyes looked like they were about to pop out of her head, but just then I heard Zoe's frantic beeping and was already heading back down through the gnome-infested garden.

"Just hand him the letter when you see him, yeah?"

Mrs. F. nodded, and I hurried back to grab my bag and get into Zoe's car.

The journey to Oxford normally took only fifty minutes but the traffic was bad, and we made painfully slow progress. I couldn't worry about that now, though. I had far more important things on my mind. I stared out the window and dug my fingernails hard into my palms. It didn't make me feel any better, but it helped to keep me from grabbing the door handle and throwing myself out of the car before lumbering back to Reading.

The medical was a long ordeal of prodding, poking and intrusive questions before I was proclaimed fit for surgery. I asked and was told that my benefactor was a healthy, heart-beating donor—the very best kind, as he or she was brain-dead, but the body was still alive, so the organs would be as fresh as possible. Most likely it was the result of a car crash, although they weren't allowed to tell me anything about how the unlucky person died. I tried to quell the thought that it was like choosing the freshest cut of meat in the supermarket, but I wasn't very successful.

The wait for the cross-match was even more tense than the medical, possibly because there was nothing to distract me from the wait. I couldn't even amuse myself by scalding my palate on a cup of hospital vending-machine tea, what with my nil-by-mouth status.

Zoe and I were sitting there in the waiting room, side by side, when I remembered my phone. I'd turned it off when entering the hospital, as per the rules, so there was no chance of a message just yet. I handed it to Zoe, and she gave me a quizzical look.

"Could you take it home with you tonight and check for any messages?"

"I'm not going to be going home."

"Zoe!"

"What? You're the only family I've got. I'm not going to leave you here until I know you're stable."

"You need your sleep."

"I wouldn't be able to sleep not knowing how you're doing."

She'd always been strong willed, so I knew I wouldn't be able to win this one.

"Okay. Well, can you at least go out for a stroll and check the messages later?"

"Can't it wait? Work's not that important right now."

"It's not work. It's personal."

"Personal? Since when have you had a personal life?"

I felt my face heat, remembering how Ollie had looked on his knees at my feet. Had that really been only a few hours ago?

"It's him, isn't it? That Ollie kid."

"He's not a kid."

"He's about my age."

"You're my sister, not my daughter."

I regretted the thoughtless words instantly as Zoe's face started to crumple. "I know. I just...I can't help it. I don't want to lose you." She wrapped her arms around me and knocked the air out of my lungs.

Understanding dawned. It wasn't so much Ollie's age that was the issue. She'd been like this after Mum and Dad died—clinging to me ferociously like I was going to disappear if she let me out of her sight. "You won't lose me, silly. Even if I'm with someone, I'll still love you just as much."

"I know, I know. I'm sorry. I'm just being selfish."

"Shush now. It's okay, it's okay." I rocked her for a while, like I had all those years ago, and it seemed to comfort her again. Eventually, she sniffed and eased her grip on me.

"You all right, Zo-Zo?"

She smiled at the old nickname, then took up my phone, promising to check the messages every couple of hours.

My eyes were following the pattern on the lino for the

umpteenth time when the surgeon approached, a porter pushing a wheelchair in his wake. We were a good enough match to proceed, me and my brain-dead donor. It made me shudder to think that there would soon be a part of that nameless victim inside me. Two parts, in fact. It was more intimate than anything I'd yet done with Ollie, and the thought made my stomach clench.

Zoe squeezed my hand as I sat down in the wheelchair. Her eyes glimmered with tears, and she gave me a tremulous smile.

"You're in good hands, Benji. Everything's going to be fine, all right?"

She seemed to need the reassurance more than I did, so I smiled and nodded, squeezing her hand back before the porter spun the chair around and wheeled me off to theatre.

# Chapter Eight

I could hear a voice somewhere. It echoed, but I wasn't all that interested in following it. I was warm and cosy, wrapped up in a red-tinged darkness. I drifted.

Sometimes, beeps washed over me, and prickles of pain made me aware of my body. I didn't want to inhabit it again right now. Things were calm, like I was bundled up in a cloud of cotton wool and hidden away from the world.

"Benji? Are you awake?"

I sighed and took possession of my body once more. I cracked my gritty eyes open and blinked at the bright lights. Pain stabbed through me as I coughed. It felt like I'd had a boulder dropped onto my belly. I didn't want to look down.

"Benji!"

I turned my head towards Zoe and was rewarded with not only a dizzying wave of nausea but the sound of her bursting into tears.

"I'm okay," I tried to say, but my mouth was so dry I could barely form the words. I managed to get my eyes to focus on the room and saw Zoe's head buried on the mattress next to me. She looked up, her eyes bloodshot and snot bubbling out of her nose.

"Hey." I smiled at her.

"Hey, yourself." She smiled back, then giggled as she wiped away the mess on her face. "How are you feeling?"

Would "like shit" be a helpful answer? It was all academic anyway, because the moment I tried speaking, my voice cracked. I couldn't seem to summon up any saliva to ease my speech, and I gave Zoe what I thought was an imploring look. "Water?" I whispered, hoping she would understand.

She sucked her lips in and shook her head. "Sorry, Benj. No can do. They said you'll be allowed fluids tomorrow, but nothing until then."

Bastards! I wanted to glare at the nurse when she came over to check up on me, but my eyes slipped closed again as the warm darkness claimed me.

As I drifted in and out of consciousness over the next few hours, I heard Zoe's voice reading to me. It sounded like it was articles from one of her celebrity gossip magazines. My sleep was populated by hunky footballers and their stick insect wives, kitten-heel shoes and plastic surgery disasters. I had a brief moment of clarity when I recalled that I hadn't managed to pack any of my own reading material because I'd been distracted by writing the note for Ollie. I wondered where he was. I'd have to ask Zoe to find him for me.

I wanted him at my bedside.

I woke again to sunlight streaming through the tall window into my private room. Zoe was by my side in an instant, the smile on her face lifting my spirits, despite my body feeling like I'd been beaten within an inch of my life.

"Morning," she said. "You're looking better today."

I tried to greet her, but if anything, my mouth was even

drier than yesterday. I licked my lips in vain, my dry tongue rasping over the cracked skin. There was a sharp sting, and I tasted the metallic tang of blood, but the pain couldn't compete with the dull throbbing in my abdomen. I attempted to lift my head so I could get a look at what they'd done to me, but my neck muscles didn't want to cooperate. I lifted a heavy hand to beckon Zoe over, then saw the cannula in there and dropped it back onto the mattress.

"Here, I'm allowed to give you some of this today."

I couldn't focus on whatever it was Zoe was showing me. It looked like a kid's lollipop made out of something spongy. I wasn't sure if I wanted it as I didn't think I had enough saliva to manage a lick. But then Zoe put the thing in my mouth, and I sucked the cool water from the sponge. My mouth zinged with the sensation, and I could move my tongue comfortably again.

"More," I said in a hoarse croak. I wanted to feel water running down my throat, soothing the raw pain there.

"Um, you'll have to ask the nurse. He said I was only to give you one, no matter how much you complained. You want me to fetch him now?"

I shook my head. "Where's Ollie?"

Zoe looked away. "I don't know."

"What?" Why didn't she know? He must have had my message by now.

"He hasn't phoned, Benj. I'm sorry."

Why wouldn't he have phoned? I tried to tell myself he simply hadn't had the message yet. Maybe Mrs. F. had missed him when he called round. Maybe he'd been delayed for some reason and never even made it.

But another, sickening possibility rose up inside me on a swell of bitter foreboding. He'd said he'd have to drive like a maniac. What if he'd had a crash. What if...

What if that was Ollie inside me?

I don't remember much after that. Someone said something about a sedative, but I wasn't paying attention. It was probably the drugs screwing with my reasoning, but I'd gone from foreboding to certainty, and collided with more despair than I'd ever imagined existed. I let it pull me under, drowning me in darkness and blotting out everything else.

Pulling me back to my darkest moment.

The lights strobed over the dance floor, whirling and leaving trails across my vision. I wondered if there'd been anything different in that last lot of coke I'd scored, and decided if there had been, I rather liked it.

The lad leaning against the bar next to me had a great arse. I ran a hand down his back and rested it there, admiring the way it made a shelf for my hand. He turned to look at me, and I nearly laughed at the orange spray-on tan he'd used. It was a classic home-job, complete with uneven lines at the jaw and white patches behind the ears. Jesus, couldn't he afford a trip to a proper tanning salon?

But then what did his face matter?

"You've got a great arse there," I said, squeezing it for emphasis. "I'd like to get to know it better."

Tan-boy leered, and I didn't even have to buy him a drink before he let me lead him to the toilets. It was still early enough that there were a couple of stalls free, so I pushed him in and down onto his knees on the hard floor.

I leaned back against the wall, enjoying his hot breath on my stomach as he quickly unzipped me. He had good technique—knew when to suck hard and when to hold back—and although it made him gag a little, he could take me all the way to the back of his throat.

My ears throbbed in time to the bassline that permeated the whole club. I looked up at the ceiling, and the light there was pulsing. My heartbeat kept the same rhythm, a frantic pounding like the one I was about to give Tan-boy.

But I wasn't, was I? My softening dick slipped out of his lips, and my head tilted sideways, like the muscles in my neck had given up. *I haven't come yet,* I wanted to scream, but my throat wasn't working. The walls expanded and contracted like my lungs refused to. Darkness fuzzed the edges of my vision, narrowing everything to an orange face, staring at me with panic in its eyes.

They found me passed out on the floor after Tan-boy fled, taking with him my wallet and remaining bag of "coke". I was rushed to hospital and spent two weeks in intensive care as my kidneys decided to give up the ghost, poisoned by whatever had been in that white powder.

Then the police arrived at my hospital bedside to tell me my wallet had been found in the pocket of a dead man, overdosed on a lethal cocktail of drugs in his shitty little bedsit. I wanted to die too. It had been the worst moment in my entire life. Blacker even than my parents dying, because this time, I knew it was my fault. I was responsible for that young man's death, and I'd never even taken the time to learn his name. I knew it now, but it was too bloody late.

The worst moment ever.

Until now.

# Chapter Nine

I glanced at the twenty millilitre cup of water in front of me. I knew I should drink it, but I just couldn't summon up the energy to lift my hand. What was the point?

I was dimly aware of an argument taking place down the hall. I tuned out the raised voices. I'd insisted that Zoe go home and get some rest, but my reasons were purely selfish. I just wanted some time alone to wallow in my misery and not have to field questions about how I was feeling.

I was feeling numb, all except for my guts, which throbbed with a dull ache.

The door swung open, and a nurse peered in at me. At least, I assume she was a nurse. Her lavender-coloured outfit looked a little too much like pyjamas for me to tell for sure, although I had noticed that at this hospital they seemed to encourage the staff to wear outlandishly coloured scrubs. She cleared her throat, looking confused and a little pissed off.

"Ben, isn't it?"

I nodded once. Not more tests. I didn't think I could face them. On the other hand, maybe it was more drugs. I wouldn't mind some more of that stuff they'd knocked me out with this morning. It would be good to get the bed lowered again too. This enforced sitting was tiring me out.

"I've got a young man demanding to be let in to see you.

Says his name is Brian Jones. He's not on the list your sister left with us."

I tried to remember if I'd ever known a Brian well enough to have him visit but drew up a blank. I didn't care enough to make any more of a response than a shrug. Then I wished I hadn't, as the motion pulled the stitches in my belly and reminded me of what was in there. Pieces of Ollie, cut out of him and pasted into me like a macabre collage. I wanted to be sick again.

Maybe if I drank the water, I could throw that up.

"He *says* he's your boyfriend," the nurse said, frowning at me. "Bright red hair?"

I definitely would remember having a redheaded boyfriend named Brian, wouldn't I? God, unless I was suffering from some bizarre amnesia and I'd made up all that stuff about me getting it on with the delivery guy. Did I have a normal life waiting for me somewhere? I stared at the nurse, willing her to tell me that I didn't need to feel this anguish, that it was all a bittersweet dream and I'd soon forget all about Ollie and the way he made me feel.

But I didn't want to forget him. Not when he'd made me feel something I'd never dared hope for. Maybe the pain was worth it, somehow.

The nurse was heading out of the room. "I'll tell him to leave, then." She turned back when halfway out of the door and frowned again. "Wait, he said to tell you he'd come to deliver more comics. Said you'd know what he meant."

I gaped. Hope sparked inside me, so bright it was painful. I felt like I was teetering on the edge of a precipice, that thread of hope holding me up above the darkness.

"Let him in."

Boyfriend...comics...Brian...red hair... It didn't add up, so I told my brain to take a hike and stared at the door as it slowly swung shut behind the nurse.

Then I heard a voice outside that made my heart leap. "I told you, he knows me as Ollie."

"If he really is your *boyfriend*, then I don't see why he wouldn't recognise your real name," the nurse replied haughtily.

The door crashed open as a vision in red and black barrelled through it.

"Ben! You would not believe the time I've had trying to find you!"

I barely had time to focus on the rapidly moving body before he was on me and my lips were ambushed. His exuberance startled me, but I opened my mouth to the messy kiss. He bathed my parched mouth in saliva, and it tasted amazing—all coffee and chocolate like the previous day. Was it really only a day? I felt like I'd lived a lifetime since our tryst in the kitchen.

His hands grasped the sides of my head, and he pulled back, flashing me a brilliant grin. I was too dazed to smile back but kept running my gaze over his face, trying to convince myself that this was real. That Ollie was here. That he was my...boyfriend?

I felt the smile start deep inside me, blotting out the pain as it rose up towards my face.

"Are you all right?" he asked me. "What happened? I was so worried, I couldn't sleep last night."

"*You* were worried?" I wanted to say, but my voice cracked. Then Ollie was holding that tiny little plastic cup up to my lips, and I gulped down my water ration. It was sweet, but not as sweet as Ollie's mouth.

I started laughing. God, that hurt. Tears ran out of my eyes, but it was almost impossible to stop. Eventually I wheezed to a halt, and the tearing on my stitches eased. I clicked my morphine button in the hope of some more being sent down the drip feed.

Ollie looked at me like I was certifiable. My gaze drifted up to his hair.

"She said you were a redhead called Brian. I thought I must have had amnesia." It was the most words I'd said in one go since the surgery. That water must have really helped. Or maybe it was just the joy of having Ollie here, alive and whole.

"Oh yeah. Uh, about that..." Ollie flushed, his face almost matching the vibrant crimson of his new dye-job. "My mates all call me Ollie after the skateboarding trick. I was never that keen on my real name, so I use it all the time now. Only my mum ever calls me Brian."

"You must be good." Ollie gave me a puzzled look. "At skating."

He dropped his eyes and shook his head. When he looked back up, there was a softness in his expression that made me want to kiss him all over again. Shame I was in too much pain to sit up that far.

"Nah, I've got the energy but not the precision. Took me a whole summer holiday to get the hang of an ollie, and I still bollocks it up half the time. That's why they called me it, you know? Just taking the piss, like mates do."

I was going to have to admit my ignorance. "What's an ollie?"

Ollie enthused. "It's like, the foundation of most other tricks, but it's bloody hard to learn. You basically start on the ground and make the board jump. That bit's tricky enough, but then you've gotta land without falling off. I'll show you sometime, when you're out of here."

I had to mentally readjust my vision of Ollie as a skateboarding pro. Something about the idea of him getting back onto the board after all those falls really appealed to me, though. His persistence was endearing. I could definitely learn something from him.

"I thought you were dead," I told him.

"Why on earth would you think that? I thought you'd been abducted by aliens or something, just taking off like that and not even leaving a note."

"I did! With Mrs. F. You know, the gnome lady."

"I didn't see her." Ollie frowned, and I wanted to wipe the furrow from his brow, but my hand was still too sodding weak to attempt it.

"So, go on, then. What's the story? They wouldn't tell me when I phoned up, but this is the transplant ward, right?"

"Yeah. I had a new kidney and pancreas put in." I frowned at him, remembering. "That bitch! I can't believe she didn't give you the note."

"She'd probably just had to pop out or something. I'm sure if she'd been in, she'd have heard me pounding on the door and seen me peering in through all your windows."

"She'd probably have phoned the police if she had. Bloody busybody."

Ollie frowned at me. "I'm sure she means well enough."

I decided I didn't want to tell him about Mrs. Felpersham's homophobia right now. Let him think the best of everyone if it made him happy. He'd learn soon enough.

"How did you find me in the end?" I asked, changing the subject.

"I didn't think you'd have stood me up, so I was pretty

worried. Thought maybe you'd had another attack. Phoned round all the A&E departments I could think of. It wasn't till this morning I had the idea of trying the kidney wards."

"Not just a pretty face, are you?"

Ollie grinned. "Nah, the rest of me's pretty too. You'll find out soon enough."

"I hope you're not expecting any action right now. I'll be out of order for a while."

"Bummer." Ollie's face fell, but then changed again as a new idea flitted through his brain. It was making me tired just watching him. I wondered what it must be like to experience life as a constant flicker of new emotions and ideas.

He pulled a packet of Malteasers out of his pocket. "Sorry, d'you mind if I have something to eat? Couldn't manage any breakfast, I was so worried."

I fought back the paternal urge to lecture him on how chocolates weren't a proper breakfast and settled instead for watching him pop the Malteasers into his mouth one by one. If I was lucky, I'd get a few spoonfuls of mashed potato and apple sauce later. I wondered if I'd enjoy them the way Ollie was relishing his chocolate.

"Nice room you've got here," he said around a mouthful of chocolate.

"It's okay." To be honest, I hadn't noticed anything about it, being too wrapped up in my own head, but I looked around to try and work out whether Ollie was simply making polite conversation. It had all the usual hospital equipment attached to the walls, but at least they were a restful mauve, and the tall window let out onto a courtyard with a large bronze sculpture in the centre. I wondered how long it would be before I was turfed out of here and onto a ward.

When Ollie had finished, he screwed up the wrapper,

shoved it back in his pocket and gave me a long stare.

"You said you thought I was dead."

"Oh, uh, yeah." It seemed so silly now, to have leapt to that assumption. "I thought you must have had an accident, when you didn't phone."

"Jesus, I thought I was the drama queen."

"Hey, I was on some pretty strong medication." I wasn't about to tell him that the last time I'd had a blowjob, the guy had died shortly afterwards. He didn't need to know all my dark secrets.

"Yeah, I guess that could screw with your thinking." Ollie glanced around the room. "Where's your sister? Thought she'd be here with you."

"She was. She's getting some rest." I thought back to Zoe's objections to Ollie. "How old are you, anyway?"

Ollie gave a sheepish grin. "I'll be twenty-one next month, but I still get ID-d all the time."

"So you're twenty?" It was better than it could have been, I suppose. I mentally calculated the difference in our ages, wondering if it was enough to be accused of cradle-snatching.

"You're thinking you're too old for me now, aren't you?" He said it with a teasing smile, but I flushed with guilt.

"I'm thirty-three," I protested. Not quite old enough to be his dad, perhaps, but close to it. I'd been as good as a dad to Zoe, after all, and she was a year older than him.

Ollie didn't seem remotely bothered, though. He gave me a sunny grin that made my heart want to somersault, although it decided not to in deference to my battered insides and settled for a celebratory wiggle.

"I like that about you," he said. "You're so much more mature than my last boyfriend was. You treat me with respect.

Take things slow. All he ever wanted me to do was bend over for him." He pursed his lips in a moue. "And do the dishes."

Could it be true? Could it be that the very thing I'd been cursing these last few years—my physical decline and loss of libido—had been part of what drew Ollie to me? What led him to seduce me? I looked down at my abdomen with a mix of nostalgia and regret. There wouldn't be any seducing going on for a while, that was for sure. I had some serious healing to do first. I'd just better hope he was still into me when I was all healthy and catheter-free again.

Ollie's smile broke out again. "I was a bit late yesterday, anyway," he said. "Wanted to redo the hair as a surprise. And then I drew something for you." He lifted up a bag and undid the buckles. It was one of those canvas bags the weird kids at school always used to carry, and like theirs, it was covered in hand-painted graffiti. Alien warriors seemed to be doing battle with a plethora of band names I'd never heard of. Ollie pulled out a plastic file, and his cheeks flushed a little as he handed it over.

"I'm gonna write the whole adventure, but so far I've only had time for the last scene. It's Cyber-Ben and Sidekick-Ollie, celebrating Cyber-Ben's escape from certain death with some life-affirming action."

He helped me to open the elastic fastenings on the file as my arms were still pretty weak. I thought I caught a glimmer of something in his eyes when he got a good look at the cannula in the back of my hand, but he just stroked the skin next to it and didn't say anything.

Then my attention was hijacked by the drawing, and everything else was shoved out of the way. I stared in disbelief, running my gaze over the inked picture. The stunningly explicit, inked picture. I raised my eyes to Ollie, not sure what to say.

"Shit, I'm sorry. I just thought, as you liked porn and comics, you might—" He chewed on his lips and reached out for the paper.

I moved it away from him. "Uh-uh. Just give me a minute. This is...amazing."

And it was. I was no expert on art, but the quality of the illustration was apparent even to me. One of the characters was lying back on a chair of some sort—from the background details it appeared they were in a spaceship—with a lascivious grin on his face. He was naked, except for a thick pelt of chest hair and a few pipes and cables that sprang out of his abdomen before disappearing inside again. He held his enormous cock at the base with one hand while the other guy lowered himself down onto it.

He was skinnier, the bottom—skinny and tattooed with spiky hair, a ring through his left nipple, and one of those weird ear-piercings like Ollie's. There was an expression of pure ecstasy on his face as his huge dick dribbled pre-come onto the other guy's belly. I looked up at Ollie, then back down at the picture. I could see him there. I could remember that blissed-out look on his face as he shot over my jeans the previous day.

I had problems seeing me as the top, though. "I'm not *that* big," I protested, then wanted to kick myself as I'd meant to say what a fantastic drawing it was.

Ollie didn't seem bothered, though. "You felt like it when you were in my mouth," he said and winked at me. "I bet you'll feel that big when we get to do this too."

There was no justice in this world. I'd just been given the hottest picture ever, drawn especially for me by my new boyfriend, and I was in no fit state to get hard. I couldn't even laugh about it without agonising pain. In the end, I just smiled.

"Kiss me," I whispered.

"I thought you'd never ask." Ollie obliged, kissing me with a slow but deliberate sensuality, unlike his previous tonsil attacks. The taste of him stimulated my appetite. I wanted to get better. I wanted to eat, I wanted to drink, I wanted to chase him around and tackle him to the ground and fuck him senseless. I wanted to spend my evenings getting to know him better. I wanted to spend long nights in his arms.

I heard someone clearing her throat at the door. Ollie gave my lower lip a little suck as he pulled away, then moved out of my line of sight so I could see the pinched-face nurse at the door.

"Visiting hours are almost over. You need your rest." She gave us both a pointed stare before moving off to the next victim.

"I'll be back later, yeah? Evening visiting hours. Or will you want your sister here instead?"

"I want you both here," I said.

"Great. She seems cool." He gave me a warm smile. "Laters, yeah?"

I tried to give him back the drawing.

"No, you keep that. I've got it scanned into the Mac, so I'll print out a colourised version for you when I get the chance. This is to remind you what you have to look forward to when you get better, yeah?"

I nodded and watched that cute little arse as he walked towards the door. I didn't need to try and hide the fact I was checking him out anymore, did I? My boyfriend. My very much alive-and-kicking boyfriend.

After he'd left, I studied the drawing for ages, only hiding it back in the file when the nurses came in on their rounds. It was a reminder that I hadn't hallucinated Ollie's visit, but also, I was captivated by Ollie's vision of me. Cyber-Ben was large but powerful. I was reminded of some of the blokes I used to watch in the clubs, studying them for tips on how to approach a potential hook-up.

Did Ollie really see me as one of those sexy tops? The thought warmed me through, right down to my toes.

Or maybe that was just the morphine.

# Chapter Ten

Ollie had been at my bedside every visiting session for the last two days, and I'd become utterly dependent on him to lift my mood. I'd been moved into a small ward by then, and the guy in the bed opposite was driving me nuts with his snoring all night and incessant moaning about this and that during the day. God, I hoped I never sounded like that. I made a mental note to keep a positive outlook. Should be much easier, though, after the transplant. I might have been on a drug regime to rival Michael Jackson's, but at least I wasn't going to have to deal with dialysis anymore.

But the pain, the frustration at being stuck in hospital, and the knowledge that I'd spend the rest of my life on a cocktail of powerful drugs to stop my body rejecting my new organs, all melted away with the warmth of Ollie's laugh and the light of his smile. That's why I was bereft when he told me he wouldn't be visiting the next day.

Zoe butted in. "Hey misery-guts, I've got the day off work, so I'll be here instead."

"Yeah, I s'pose." Oh God, I sounded like a sullen teenager. I tried to summon up a smile for them both. They didn't deserve me going all grumpy on them when they'd both been putting themselves out driving over here to visit every day. "What are you up to, then?" I asked Ollie. Did that sound demanding and suspicious? I didn't mean it to, but I did want to know more about his life.

Fortunately, Ollie didn't seem to find my tone objectionable. "Got my shift at the café. I can't let them down, and anyway"—he started spinning his leather bracelets around, an action I'd learnt signalled nervousness—"I, uh, need the money right now."

What for? But I didn't ask. I didn't want to be the prying, controlling type. From the few details he'd let slip, it sounded as if his ex had been like that, and I wanted to be different, to treat him with respect. "I thought you were on holiday this week," I said, trying to keep the whine out of my voice.

"Um, yeah, well, I didn't want to bother you when you were in such a mess already..." Ollie trailed off, looking at Zoe as if for help. The two of them seemed to have made friends these last couple of days. Or at least, Ollie was friends with Zoe. I couldn't yet tell what she made of him, as she was always perfectly polite yet guarded in his presence. Still, Ollie didn't seem to notice, maybe because he didn't know what she was normally like.

Ollie's imploring eyes made him look about twelve, and I wondered what on earth I thought I was doing with him. The age gap seemed insurmountable at times like this.

"Nuh-uh. You tell him yourself," Zoe said. "I'm not doing your dirty work."

Eventually he took a deep breath, and it all came out in a rush. "I-got-the-sack-'cause-I-was-late-and-one-of-your-neighbours-saw-my-van-parked-outside-your-house-for-fifteen-minutes-and-phoned-it-in-to-my-boss. Sorry, ex boss," he added sheepishly. "Turns out she's his great aunt, and she's a right curtain-twitching busybody."

"Oh," I said. Then I thought about what he was telling me.

"Shit! You mean, on Friday when we were in the kitchen..." A vision of Ollie looking up as he took my cock in his mouth momentarily distracted me. I glanced at Zoe, who was watching us both with ill-concealed interest. "And he fired you for that? Bastard!"

Ollie just shrugged. "Yeah, but it is against the rules, and he said he'd had enough of my insolent ways giving his company a bad image. Said I was guilty of *at least* seven different uniform violations." He sounded proud of this last fact.

"Did you wear that T-shirt into work, then?" Zoe asked.

Ollie looked down at his skinny-fit, purple T-shirt. It was the one I'd seen him in that time I went to spy at the skate park. Turns out the rhinestones spelt out: *Drama Queen, fuelled by chocolate*. I couldn't imagine the confidence it must take to walk out wearing something like that. Especially as it was quite clearly a girl's T-shirt. Looked good on him, though, and the slogan was particularly apt as he always seemed to have a bag of Malteasers or M&Ms on the go. God knew how someone who ate that much chocolate could stay so skinny.

"Nah, this one's way too good for work. He mostly had a problem with the hair and the jewellery. Said I looked like a punk, but so what? Didn't make any difference to how well I could deliver a bloody parcel, did it? And none of the customers ever seemed bothered."

"What a git!" Zoe exclaimed. "After you saving Ben's life on the doorstep last week! Now that's customer service."

Ollie looked alarmed. "You wouldn't have died, would you?"

I shook my head. "Not when Zoe was coming to check up on me."

Ollie nodded, but from the way his gaze fixed on me, I knew he was still worried. I needed to change the subject from my ill health before it scared him off for good.

I considered the situation from Ollie's point of view. "So, are you looking for another job, then? Or are they giving you more shifts at the café?"

The bracelets started spinning again. "Not exactly." I waited for him to continue. When he eventually did, there was a nervous smile on his face. "I've been looking into setting up that café I told you about. In the park, by the ramps?" I flushed, remembering spying on him there. Ollie continued. "There's this building there that's been empty for years. It's just perfect, and the rent seems pretty cheap, but there's so much I need to sort out, and I'm not sure how to. I've been researching suppliers and shit, but I don't know how to put a business plan together, and I need to have one to apply for a loan."

"You really want to run a café?" Zoe asked. She sounded perfectly polite to the untrained ear, but I could hear the scepticism lurking under her innocent question. "Catering is bloody hard work, you know."

"Yeah, it'd be brilliant. I'd be my own boss, get to chat to people all day, make good food and drinks. An' what's more, I'd be able to watch the skaters, but I wouldn't feel I had to get up there and prove anything. You know, that I'm still tough even though I'm a poof. I could just be a spectator." He grinned and pulled up a sleeve to show us a skinned elbow. "Could do without getting these all the time."

I hated the idea of him hurting himself just to prove a point to his so-called friends. As I stared at Ollie's broken skin, a plan formed. I'd need my laptop, but until I could get Zoe to bring it in, paper and pen would suffice.

"So, this park, does it get busy? You think you'll have enough customers? I can't imagine teenagers have all that much money to spend."

"You'd be surprised. Most of 'em come from nice families.

You know, their dads drive BMWs and Mercs. They've got a fair bit to waste on cans of Coke and chocolate from the nearby shops. I reckon I can persuade them to come and buy stuff from me instead, especially if I can give them somewhere warm to sit on chilly days. Play some decent music." I frowned, but Ollie was determined to sell the idea to me. "It's not just them, though. During the day, the park is packed with mums and littl'uns. I could serve tea and coffee and cake. Maybe get some organic baby foods in. Keep some toys in the corner. And then when the weather's hot, in the school holidays, I reckon I could sell enough ice creams to keep me in business all year round."

"What about bad weather? And will you be able to manage all of this by yourself? What about if you get sick?"

"That's the beauty of it, you see. When it's quiet, I'll be able to get on with my illustrations, and then when it gets really busy, I can take on extra help. My cousin said she'd give me a few hours' help every Saturday, and she's brilliant with people." Ollie's cheeks dimpled as he launched into his plans. Okay, so he didn't have a clue about the administrative side of running a business, but he had good ideas and a surplus of energy and enthusiasm. I watched the way his hands moved to emphasise his words, and I realised that I didn't want him to ever lose that optimism. I wanted to help him make his dreams come true.

I just had to hope he'd still want me along for the ride when they did.

In the end, it was Ollie who drove me home. Zoe had been at work when the doctor discharged me, but Ollie was right there with me. He cleared out the bedside cabinet while I signed the paperwork and accepted my Ziploc bag full of medication. There was one of those day-of-the-week pill containers in there, with a separate compartment for each day. I was going to have to take three different immunosuppressant drugs three times a day for at least the first six months, and two of them I'd remain taking for as long as my new organs lasted. The list of possible side effects was about as long as my arm and just about the scariest thing I'd ever read. Still, better that than have my body reject the transplants, I suppose.

I wasn't too thrilled about erectile dysfunction appearing on all three lists, although come to think of it, I'd been told not to have sex for a month anyway. The doctor wasn't too detailed about what was included in that definition, though, but as I didn't particularly want to discuss the ins and outs of my sexual preferences with the guy, I decided it probably ruled out everything.

Well, mostly everything. Maybe I could think of a few ways to get Ollie off, even if my orgasms were out of bounds.

"I've got your bag," Ollie said when I went to pick it up.

"I can manage. I'm not a total invalid."

Ollie gave me this look of bemused pity. "You know you're not meant to be lifting anything until your muscles have healed. Anyway, there's a porter waiting outside with a wheelchair."

"I don't need a sodding wheelchair."

"Right. Because after all the exercise you've had this last week of lying on your arse, you're ready for a half-a-mile walk across the hospital to get to the car park."

He had me there. I'm sure it hadn't been that far away when I arrived, but then maybe Zoe had lucked out with the parking. I submitted to the chair with rather ill grace, I admit, but I was secretly glad not to have to prove my level of fitness...or unfitness, as was more likely.

I was silent during the trip down the hospital corridors, listening to Ollie chat to the porter about whether he enjoyed his job and whether he had any family.

"Five beautiful girls and a handsome baby boy," the man answered in heavily accented English. I could believe his kids would be attractive, as the man himself was so striking. Tall and dark-skinned, he looked like he'd have fit in better modelling than working as a lowly porter, if it weren't for the gold tooth and long dreadlocks hanging down his back.

"You got kids yourself?" he asked.

I could hear Ollie's grin in the sound of his voice. "Nah, not much chance of that. I've got a little brother, though. He's a right little bruiser. Reckon he takes after his dad."

"I didn't know you had a brother," I said, aggrieved he'd confided in the porter before me.

"Well, half-brother. I don't see him as often as I'd like."

After that, the two of them got back to the porter's brood, while I sat and pondered how much I really knew about Ollie. Clearly there were big gaps in my knowledge that needed filling.

Ollie's car was one of them.

I stared at it, blinking, forcing myself not to react visibly to the rust patches, gaffa tape around the wing-mirror and heap of discarded chocolate wrappers and take-away coffee containers that littered the inside. Worse yet, it was a white Fiat Panda—a car that not only looked like a piece of shit but had virtually no acceleration and was cramped inside.

Ollie swung open the passenger door with a flourish.

"Your carriage awaits you, sir."

"Thanks." I lowered myself into the seat and got a lungful of air-freshener from the cardboard Christmas tree hanging from the rear view mirror. Now that I was inside, I could see a few touches that were more obviously Ollie, such as the row of miniature skateboards blu-tacked to the dashboard, and the

R2-D2 keyring hanging next to that stinky air-freshener tree.

"What d'you reckon?" Ollie said as he thunked down into the driver's seat, making the whole car shake. "I know she doesn't look much yet, but she's all mine. I saved up out of my wages."

He sounded so proud of himself, I couldn't help smiling. I remembered my first car, a beat-up old Vauxhall Astra, and how good it felt to have finally gained a bit of independence. That feeling soured when, five months later, Mum and Dad had their crash, but I'd had to keep driving so I could take Zoe places in my new role as legal guardian.

"She's lovely," I lied, patting the dashboard. "Does she have a name?"

Ollie turned the key, and as the starter motor struggled, he flashed me a bashful grin. "Rogue." He gave her some choke, and she finally caught. "Not sure if I've cursed her with that name, but I reckon it suits her."

As Ollie negotiated his way through the maze of hospital car parks, I pondered the snippets of information I'd been picking up about his life. "So how old's your brother?" I asked.

"He's five now. Tyler, he's called. Little menace but cute as hell."

"And you share the same mother?" It was a guess. Ollie hadn't mentioned his parents much, but I had the impression they were both still alive. Maybe he was just trying not to flaunt that fact in deference to my parentless state.

"Yeah, that's right."

"Big age gap there."

"Don't," Ollie warned, but with a wry grin on his face.

"Don't what?"

"Don't you go stressing about age gaps again. We're fine."

"So long as you don't start calling me Daddy," I grumbled.

Ollie snorted. "Believe me, one dad and one stepfather is plenty for me. I'm not after another." He paused for a while at a busy junction, and I thought perhaps we were through with the subject, but then he picked it up again once we were moving.

"My dad's out in Saudi Arabia at the moment. Works for BP and spends half his time in oil-producing countries. That's what drove Mum crazy in the end. They got divorced when I was fifteen, and by the time I was sixteen, she'd already married Terrence and was pregnant with Tyler."

"Fast work."

"Yeah. Turned out she'd been seeing him for years when Dad was away, but they didn't make anything official until Terrence divorced his wife."

Ollie's tone was conversational, but I could see the tension in his jaw muscles.

"Do you get on with Terrence?"

His shrug said it all. "We got on okay to begin with, but he couldn't deal with me coming out. Didn't want his baby growing up in the same house as a batty boy."

"He told you that?" My hands balled into fists as I imagined giving a piece of my mind to this Terrence guy.

"Nah, not in so many words, but it was pretty obvious, if you know what I mean. His mates were worse. They think I can't understand it when they talk in patois, but I picked up a fair bit."

"So you moved out as soon as you could? In with your friend Omar?"

"Didn't want to be where I wasn't wanted."

It wasn't exactly answering the question, and I had the feeling Ollie was holding something back, but I didn't pry. He'd tell me in his own time. Instead, I reached over and squeezed his thigh gently. Ollie took his eyes off the Oxford traffic for a brief moment and smiled at me. Somehow I didn't think I'd ever get tired of those smiles. They ran the gamut from exuberant to subtle, and this one was tinged with a kind of sad gratitude.

I was quiet for the rest of the journey, saving my strength so that I could make Ollie feel welcome and wanted when we got back home.

# Chapter Eleven

Zoe was waiting for us back at the flat. God, it was good to be home. I sank back onto my living room sofa and propped my feet up on the coffee table. Ah, bliss!

"Okay, your fridge and freezer are stocked with meals that fit the new diet sheet." Zoe brandished a list, and once again I thanked my lucky stars that I had a chef for a sister. "You've got to remember to write down everything you eat and drink for the next few weeks, though, like that nutritionist said."

"Yep, I was listening too, thanks." It turned out that, for the moment at least, my diet was even more restricted than it had been before the operation. All that should change over the next month, though. I had the prospect of fresh coffee with sugar in to look forward to. Hell, I'd even be able have a coffee with whiskey in it. My mouth watered at the thought.

The front door slammed shut, and footsteps bounced up the hall.

"All done," Ollie announced and threw himself down next to me. "God, I'm knackered. I bet I stink." He'd been shifting all the boxes of unused dialysate out into the garage, ready for collection. It was good to see the back of the bloody things.

"Come here, you." I pulled Ollie over to me and kissed him lavishly. He didn't stink, but he was ripe with the scent of fresh sweat and young male. It was one of the best smells in the world, and it was a bugger that I still couldn't seem to get it up, although maybe that was for the best. I wouldn't want to rip my stitches doing anything too strenuous, and I'd had those stern instructions not to have any sex for the next four weeks.

"Can't wait to get you alone," he whispered in my ear.

Anxiety rippled through me. I hadn't yet told him what the doctor had advised as far as "sexual relations" went. Ollie had been supplying me with a steady stream of hand-drawn porn, and I could tell that he was expecting something from me now we had a bit of privacy. Thank God Zoe was still in the room.

"I'll see myself out then, shall I?" Zoe said. "Doesn't look like there's anything else I can do for you. Ollie seems to have it all under control." I definitely wasn't imagining the dryness of her tone.

I leant sideways—I could do that now the scars were starting to heal—and pleaded with my eyes.

"Why not stay for a cuppa?"

Ollie pouted at me but hid it from Zoe. Then that brilliant smile was back as he turned and offered to put the kettle on.

"No, really. I'm due at work any minute now, and I'm sure you two boys would rather be alone. I'll see you tomorrow, Benji." She bent down to kiss the top of my head. "You too, Ollie. Look after him for me."

Ollie grinned, grabbed hold of Zoe, and planted a sloppy kiss right on her lips. I swear she blushed. Zoe never blushes.

She trotted out of the room, and moments later, I heard the front door slam.

And then we were alone.

"So, how about that cup of tea, then?" I made a move to get up, but it still took me a while to rise, and Ollie put out a hand to stop me. It didn't take much to overpower me, but I was determined to get my strength back. It might take the best part of a year, but I was going to work out and get so as I could fit back into all my old clothing. I was going to get me a body I could be proud of again. One that would drive Ollie wild with desire, and hopefully by then I'd be in a fit state to do something about it.

"How about we find some other form of refreshments?" he asked, his eyes twinkling. "You're looking pretty tasty to me right now." He licked my earlobe and swung his leg over me so that he was sitting astride my lap.

I groaned. It was hard to believe he could find me attractive like this, but the way he nuzzled into my neck seemed to confirm that he did. No, scratch that. The way his erection was digging into my stomach definitely confirmed it. I hissed as he shifted and his dick nudged me right in the sensitive area around my scar.

"Shit! I'm sorry. Did I hurt you?"

"Just a bit. I'll be okay." I put my hand to my belly in a protective gesture.

Ollie gave me a strange look. "So, now we're alone and all..." He looked uncertain and so young that I started worrying about cradle-snatching again. Maybe all that talk about his ex had been bullshit. God, I hoped not. I didn't think I could handle the responsibility of being his first—not in my condition—although on the other hand, at least he wouldn't have anyone to compare me unfavourably to.

"I'm not expecting anything," I said, trying to sound generous rather than dismissive. "Not sure if I can manage anything anyway. Not after the surgery and all these drugs they've got me on."

Ollie shook his head vehemently. "That's not what I meant. I wondered if...if I could see it now. The scar."

Oh. That's what he was after. Shit. I broke out in a sweat. "It's not pretty."

He shrugged. "You think I care about that?"

I stalled. "I've still got the tube as well. They won't take it out for another few months, until they're sure everything's working okay with the new kidney."

"Are you gonna let me see? I mean, it's okay if you need more time and all, but seeing as how loads of doctors and nurses have seen it, I don't see why you should be so worried about me having a look." Ollie pouted.

"I didn't care about what they thought of me," I said, then gulped, astonished at my honesty.

Ollie gave me a soft smile. "Haven't I told you scars are sexy?"

He had, but there was a world of difference between the battle wounds on his illustrated heroes and the surgical incision in my guts. But I nodded, because this was Ollie, and if I couldn't give back something after all the care and attention he'd given me this last week, then that would make me a selfish git. And okay, I knew that deep down I really was a selfish git, but I was determined to at least try to change, for Ollie's sake. I let out a shaky breath and tried to squash down my rising paranoia as I lifted my T-shirt, then pushed down my trackie bottoms to reveal the full extent of the scar.

Ollie gasped, and I shut my eyes. I didn't need to see my belly to know what it looked like now. There was a curved incision that started four inches to the right of my navel and ended up four inches underneath, almost in the crease of my groin. The stitches bristled like a row of blue insect legs, and the bruising spread out all around them. They'd had to shave my belly, so I looked even more patchy than usual—like a discarded teddy bear, worn bald and carelessly repaired.

"Ben? Can I... Do you mind if I touch you?"

He sounded awestruck, and I opened my eyes to find him transfixed. He didn't look disgusted, just fascinated.

"O-okay." I cleared my throat. "Be gentle."

He gave me a steady gaze. "Chill. You can trust me."

I tried to relax. I slumped back against the cushions and told my body not to tense when it felt Ollie's touch. And then there it was. The lightest of contact, his fingers barely feathering against my skin as he traced around the scar. "It's incredible to think of what you've been through," he whispered. "You're so brave."

And then he kissed me, a fleeting brush of his lips right between my bellybutton and the incision.

My eyes started to prickle. I wanted to tell him that I wasn't brave. That I'd brought all this on myself with my reckless behaviour. That I was brimming with fear and neuroses. But I couldn't seem to dredge up the words when I could feel his breath caressing my belly; when I could see him bent over me like that, loving me despite my flaws; when I could feel my body start to respond to his proximity. Just the faintest stirring of arousal, but enough to let me know that things would get better, given time.

"Come here," I rasped. "Please."

And then he was astride me, leaning his weight back onto my thighs and kissing me deeply. He'd slowed down since our first kiss in the kitchen, the sloppy enthusiasm giving way to a more controlled passion, and he moaned into my mouth, sucking my tongue hard. He sounded so turned on, so ardent, and I wanted to reward him in some way. To say thank you for sticking with me. For being here.

And more than that, I longed to taste him.

"Please," I asked as Ollie nibbled my earlobe, and I ran my hand up his leg to find his hard-on, trapped by his jeans. "Let me suck you off."

I felt his shuddering exhalation against my neck.

"You really want to?" he asked, his voice small and uncertain. I recalled then that all of his illustrations had shown the Ollie character blowing the Ben character—never the other way around. Had he never had a guy do this for him before?

"God, yes. I want to." It had been way too long since I'd tasted cock, and I'd always loved it but never felt this way about any of the guys I'd been with before. The need to feel him in my mouth was like a craving, pure and painful. Was it possible to become addicted to something you hadn't yet experienced?

Or perhaps I was just addicted to Ollie.

"How should we do this? I don't want to hurt you."

I looked into his eyes and saw the truth there. He really didn't want to hurt me in any way. He was way too good for me, but at least I could do something for him.

"Just kneel where you are."

But he lifted himself off me and began shedding his clothing. The baggy jeans dropped to the floor, along with a pair of red-and-white spotty boxers, and I got my first eyeful of a naked Ollie. Christ, he was gorgeous. Nothing like the guys in the DVDs with their six packs, bulging pecs and all-over tans, but he was lean, and his skin was creamy white, making the tattoo and the smattering of dark hair stand out vividly. And oh God, was that a ring through one of his nipples? Just like the illustrations. It was almost enough to distract me from the sight of his prick. Almost but not quite.

I hadn't had a proper look the last time, it had all been so hurried and such a surprise. Now I took my time, admiring the way his prick jutted out, smooth and pale and beautifully proportioned. He was bigger than I'd expected for a small-framed bloke. Even his balls were large and I couldn't wait to feel their weight against my palm.

I licked my dry lips. "Here." I beckoned him over, but he was already moving, settling down above me with his knees either side of my thighs, and then all I could see was Ollie filling my whole frame of vision. I could smell him too, arousal sharpening the musk of his sweat and that underlying Ollie scent—all heady sweetness.

I ran a fingertip down the treasure trail that led from his navel to his groin. So perfect. My hands explored him, stroked the velvety softness of his dick, cupped his heavy balls and rolled them. Ollie gasped, and the sound spurred me on, my touch growing more confident and firm as I remembered how to pleasure another man. I wrapped my hand around him and pumped slowly, adding a twist and squeeze at the top of each stroke, enjoying the slide of his foreskin and the way the flushed head was revealed with every down stroke. Soon a bead of precome formed, the scent overpoweringly male and delicious.

I closed my mouth over him. I hadn't meant to so soon, but I couldn't resist tasting. I moaned as the bitter-salt flavour melted over my taste-buds. I'd missed this so much, this simple pleasure. The sensation of a heavy shaft sliding over my tongue, pushing deeper and deeper into me until my lips bumped against my hand. But this wasn't just any nameless hook-up; this was Ollie. I looked up to find him watching me, one hand braced against the wall while the other reached down tentatively to stroke my hair. His lips parted as his breath came fast. Those eyes were darker than I'd ever seen them, a rich espresso, and a flush spread over his cheeks and down his neck and chest.

"Ben! That's— I've never— Fuck! Ben!"

I'd never seen anything so hot. Not in all those DVDs and Internet porn sites I'd visited. Because this was Ollie, and he was moaning my name, and he still wanted me, despite me being broken.

I gave his balls a final grope and moved my hands around to knead his buttocks, hoping I hadn't lost the knack of deep-throating through lack of practise. There was resistance in his hips when I tried to pull him in.

"Not gonna hurt you," Ollie said.

I couldn't exactly reply, but I tried to convey how much I wanted this with my eyes as I pushed forward until my nose hit his pubes and I could no longer breathe. God knows why that felt so good, that eye-watering, choking fullness, but it always did for me. There was power in taking another man that deep inside, in knowing I was capable of giving him such pleasure. And with Ollie, it was even better, feeling his thighs start to shake and hearing his incoherent pleas.

I pulled back to take a breath, then plunged down again, and this time, his hips twitched, and his fingers convulsed on my scalp, as if he was fighting the urge to thrust into me. I looked up to find an exquisite agony twisting his face. He opened his eyes and stared, perhaps shocked, as I swallowed around him.

"Ben, I'm gonna— Can't stop!"

I didn't want him to. I took one more breath and pulled him deep again, giving him everything I could with throat and tongue. He inspired me, and I wanted to see him lose it.

My finger sliding down his arse crack was what did it. I felt the trembling build, and then he froze, a look of sheer ecstasy transforming him as his balls emptied down my throat. I swallowed greedily, enjoying the sensation of his cock pulsing with every spurt, but then pulled back to breathe and to taste.

To savour his pleasure to the very last drop. I sucked him dry as he softened and whimpered, his body thrilling with the aftershocks.

He collapsed slowly, considerately, shifting back so he was sitting almost on my knees and resting his sweaty forehead against mine. I could feel the gelled spikes of his hair pricking against my skin, and I smiled. My jaw might ache like buggery, but at least it took my mind off the pain in my guts.

"Wow!" Ollie said, as if it explained everything. Perhaps it did.

I kissed his nose.

"Best. Blowjob. Ever," he said emphatically.

I grinned. "You know I'm going to have to write that down on my diet sheet now. What food group do you think I should count it as? Or is spunk a drink?"

Ollie giggled and sat up, balancing on his haunches. "I reckon it's a condiment. Put it down as Ollie's Special Sauce." His smile was teasing, but there was something oh-so-tender about his eyes. I couldn't bear looking in them as they made me feel strange inside. All light-headed and short of breath. Although that could simply have been the after-effects of my exertion.

"Can I do anything for you?" Ollie asked softly, looking down at my crotch where the outline of my dick was clearly visible through the fabric of my trackie bottoms.

I realised with amazement that I was half-hard. I also realised that I really didn't want to come. Not with my belly still healing up. The convulsions of orgasm would be hell on my damaged tissues.

"No, I'm good," I said. Ollie looked doubtful. "*I'm good!* And anyway, the doctor said no sex for a month."

"A month! That's like, *forever*!"

I couldn't help but chuckle at his crestfallen expression. "Don't worry, there'll be plenty of blowjobs and handjobs for you. I could do with the practise. I'm a bit rusty."

"That was rusty? Are you serious?"

"Oh yeah, I can do much better than that. You just wait." He'd have to wait until at least tomorrow, I thought, rubbing my jaw surreptitiously.

His forehead creased. "So, I'd be doing you a favour, right? Helping you brush up on your skills."

"That's it."

His sunny grin was back. "In that case, I think we'd better create a new column on your diet sheet."

I kissed him softly, smiling against his mouth.

# Chapter Twelve

It was amazing how different my flat felt without the boxes of dialysate everywhere. The rooms seemed lighter, brighter. Or maybe that was just the effect of having Ollie around. He made sure the blinds and curtains were all fully open and switched on my halogen spotlights whenever a cloud hid the sun. I grumbled about the electricity bill, but secretly I was glad to have him do it as it meant I had an even better view of him as he fussed over me.

Who am I trying to fool? It was brighter because his smile could outshine all the halogen lamps in the world. It was my own personal sun, and I basked in its warmth. All I wanted was to make him happy so I'd see it all the time.

I'd been home for a couple of days when I realised Ollie's café plans had hit a major obstacle. We'd spent the morning going through a long list of projected setup expenses and regular expenses for the first financial year, along with his savings and projected income, and I'd input it all onto a spreadsheet for him. Strictly speaking, I wasn't meant to be working, and James had given me a week off, with a plan to ease back into work gradually after that. But helping Ollie out didn't count as real work, did it? Not when it was so much fun seeing his eager anticipation and hearing all his plans.

Until I entered in the last formula and saw the shortfall in funds.

"Shit. Does that minus mean what I think it does?"

I nodded, and Ollie whistled through the gap in his teeth.

"So I've got to find another three grand from somewhere?"

In the larger scheme of things, it was a paltry sum, but to a twenty-year-old who worked as a barista, drove a rusty Fiat Panda, and wasn't eligible for a bank loan, it must have seemed a king's ransom.

I put the laptop on the coffee table and pulled Ollie onto my lap instead. He curled into me, and I could see his mind working away from the frown on his face.

"There's only one thing for it. I'm gonna have to get another job," he announced.

"Better make it something that pays well and doesn't take up too much of your time. I'm getting kind of attached to having you hanging around the place."

"Stripper, maybe?" Ollie smirked at me. "Or an escort? I hear they do quite well for themselves."

"You'd have to put out for middle-aged businessmen, you know."

"Good thing I've got a kink for them, then," Ollie said, kissing my jaw.

"I am not middle-aged! Jesus, you whippersnappers. You think anyone over thirty's had it, don't you?" I paused a moment. "Not that I've had any just lately, more's the pity."

Ollie kissed me some more, effectively quashing my protests. I explored his mouth in a leisurely fashion, savouring the taste of him and loving the small noises of pleasure that escaped his throat. I was such a goner.

When I pulled back for air, I knew exactly what I needed to do.

"Young man, I've succumbed to your fiendish powers of persuasion, and I'd like to invest three thousand pounds in your business. Especially if it keeps you off the game," I added.

"What, you mean...You'd do that? For me?" Ollie's eyes shone, but his face remained serious.

"I think it's a good investment, and I've got the money, so why not?"

"Yes! You are a fucking superhero!" Ollie's arms squeezed me tight, and I couldn't help hissing as he put pressure against my belly. "Sorry," he said, easing off. "I keep forgetting."

"It's okay." I kissed him again to show him it really was.

"You know you'll get it back, don't you? With interest."

"I certainly hope so." Although to be perfectly honest, I wouldn't have cared even if I never saw that money again. It was worth every penny to see the hope dancing in Ollie's eyes.

"Is there anything I can do to say thank you?" Ollie asked, and by the way his eyes drifted down to my crotch, I knew what he was contemplating.

"Not yet," I said, catching his hand as it made its way to my groin.

Ollie pouted a little, but he seemed to know better than to push past the boundaries I'd set.

"Tell you what, though, I'd love another taste of your special sauce. We could make it a celebratory one. I'll get you to go off like a bottle of bubbly."

Ollie sniggered. "So long as you don't try and stick a cork in there."

"Agreed, no corks. But I still want to see if you can hit the ceiling."

We were both chuckling as we kissed again, this time with rising passion. I felt a twinge of apprehension as I wondered what Zoe would have to say about this loan plan, but it faded away as I lost myself in exploring Ollie's mouth.

My first week at home had been a period of gradual adjustment to my new way of living, now that the tyranny of dialysis no longer ruled my life. Ollie spent as much time as he could around my place without officially moving in but was often out meeting possible suppliers for his café and investigating cheap sources of furniture and equipment. I was impressed by how quickly he'd grasped the basics of the financial plan I'd helped create, understanding the need to eke out my loan by economising. He'd been scouring eBay and the local free-ads for bargains.

One thing I insisted on was that Ollie went back home at night. It was easy to use the excuse of needing a good night's sleep while my body was healing, so I didn't have to admit how the idea of him staying over made me uneasy. Not only were there Zoe's feelings to consider—and I knew she was having difficulty dealing with me having a relationship, although she seemed to be making a real effort to befriend Ollie—but I was worried that if I grew too dependent on him being there, it would come back and bite me in the arse one day.

But while my nights were cold and lonely, my days were almost too busy. After that first week, I had started back on my own work again, picking up on the Dane Gibson Associates account I'd been handed before my transplant. I managed to fit in a fair bit of work around the daily hospital visits to check my blood creatinine levels, but I was finding it increasingly difficult to concentrate when Ollie was in the flat. Even when he was in a different room, working on his own project, I kept finding excuses to go and see him. Visits that would often end with him panting and sweaty, and me with a mouthful of something that definitely wasn't on the list of approved food and drink. My jaw muscles were getting such a workout, perhaps I really would end up looking like the lantern-jawed Cyber-Ben from Ollie's drawings.

I was pondering this as I slouched on the sofa one evening, waiting for Ollie to return from one of his missions to get hold of some arcane piece of catering equipment. I had strewn the illustrations all over the coffee table in order to study them. Not in the way I would once have done, before the surgery and drugs had demolished what was left of my libido. No, I was studying them to try and understand Ollie. I needed to know what he expected of me—of this relationship—because I was frightened of messing it all up. Unfortunately, the illustrations all showed the Ollie character either taking orders from the über-macho hero, or performing all manner of sexual favours for him. Sometimes both at once. I didn't think I could be that man for him. I didn't know if I even wanted to be. Was he still going to be willing to stick around when he discovered I wasn't the dominant hero he was hoping for?

There was a sound of a key in the door, and I didn't make an effort to get up. The half hour I'd spent cleaning the kitchen earlier had wiped me out.

Then I heard Zoe's voice.

"Hey, Benj, I found this stray hanging around the kitchens begging for scraps and thought you might like to adopt hi— Oooh, what's all this? Are these your drawings, Oll?"

I leapt up like someone had fitted my arse with springs, then doubled over with pain as my injured tissues protested.

"No," I managed to force out through panting breaths. "Don't look."

But I was too late, as Zoe had already picked one up. I

couldn't see which it was, so I concentrated on getting the rest back into the folder.

"Hey, Ollie, these are great. Filthy but great."

I looked up, worried Ollie would be pissed off that I'd left them out on display. Little bugger had a smug grin, though.

Zoe looked up from the picture with dimpled cheeks. "If this is meant to be Ben, I think you've seriously overestimated the size of his willy."

"Hey!" I protested. Okay, so I agreed with her, but I still didn't need to hear that. "When's the last time you saw it, anyway?"

Zoe rolled her eyes. "C'mon, Ben, we were living in the same house for like, years, and you *never* locked the bathroom door."

"I wasn't allowed to. In case I collapsed," I explained for Ollie's benefit. Since Social Services had been iffy about letting a teenager with diabetes take on the role of guardian, I'd had to adhere to a set of best-practise guidelines that would have made a Health and Safety inspector weep with joy.

"Can I have that back now, please?" I asked, grabbing for the paper in Zoe's hands. She let go with reluctance, then turned to Ollie.

"Could you give me and Ben a couple of minutes, hon? Make us some tea or something?"

Ollie made himself scarce, leaving me staring at Zoe with trepidation. She had her serious face on, and I wondered if I was in for a lecture on corrupting innocent young men into creating porn.

"You two seem to be getting on better these days," I said. "Have you decided the age gap isn't such a problem now?"

Zoe sighed. "He's a nice guy, Benj, but I'm worried you're

taking things too fast. What's this I hear about you lending him money?"

"That's an investment!"

"That's what he said. But don't you think it's all a bit of a coincidence? I mean, with him being so young and so all over you, even though you're ill…" She trailed off as I glared at her.

"What are you trying to say?"

She folded her arms and set her jaw. "I just don't want you being taken advantage of by a gold-digger, that's all."

"I don't believe it! Do you seriously think—" I was too angry to frame a coherent sentence.

"I'm only looking out for you." She put a hand on my arm, and I threw it off.

"I don't need you looking out for me. I'm a grown man."

"Yeah, and he's not."

I stared at her, but all I could see was genuine concern in her eyes. Fuck. I didn't need this. I really didn't need the two most important people in my life at loggerheads.

"Zo, I don't want to talk about this. Let's just pretend you never said any of it, okay?"

"Pretend what?" Ollie said, breezing into the room with a tray of tea things. He froze, obviously taking in our tense body language. "What's going on?"

For a moment, I thought Zoe was going to say something, and I put as much "don't you dare" into my expression as I could manage. She obviously remembered that from her younger years and backed down again.

Zoe gave a tight smile. "I'm off now, then. I'll leave you two together, shall I? Doesn't look like I'm needed here."

"Zoe!" I bellowed after her, but the front door was already slamming.

"What was all that about?" Ollie was the picture of bewildered consternation. "Ben? What's going on?"

I racked my brains trying to think of a reasonable explanation for Zoe's behaviour that wouldn't make Ollie feel bad. I settled for a half truth. "She's just stressed at the moment," I said. "Too much going on at work, and she's probably feeling a bit left out now she's single but I've got you. I mean, she's had me to herself all these years. It must be tough on her."

"She doesn't like me, does she?"

Ollie's expression was so forlorn, I just wanted to hug him happy again. "Believe me, you'd know it if she didn't like you. She's not one to mince her words. She's just...she's concerned that you're so much younger than me. Younger than her, even."

Ollie turned away to set down the tray on the coffee table, so I couldn't see his face as he started speaking. The dejected tone of his voice said it all, though. "Then I can't win, can I? I'll always be younger than her. Shit, Ben, I don't want to come between you and Zoe. I know how important you are to each other."

I wrapped my arms around him from behind. "You're important to me too."

"Yeah, but I've only just come along. Zoe's looked up to you like a father for years and years."

"But I'm not her dad, and even if I was, she still wouldn't have the right to choose my boyfriends for me."

"Boyfriends? You mean you have more than one?" Ollie sounded like he was trying for lighthearted banter, but I felt his body tense. Curious. He must have known there was no way I could be seeing anyone else, so why would that stray remark cause such a strong reaction?

I sought to reassure him. "You're the only boyfriend I've

ever had."

"What, seriously?" Ollie broke my hold and swivelled so he could look me in the eyes. "You're thirty-three and you've never had a boyfriend before?"

I shrugged. "It's not so strange. I've had friends with benefits. I've had one-night stands. I just never wanted a relationship with any of them. I didn't have the time when Zoe was younger; then, once she decided she was independent enough to move out, I went a bit wild for a few years."

"I can't imagine you going wild." Ollie stroked my jaw. "Must have been quite a sight. I wish I'd known you then."

I gave a grim smile. "Believe me, you don't. You wouldn't have liked me. I was in better shape, but I was a right cocky arsehole."

"Sounds like my ex," Ollie mumbled.

As I hugged Ollie tight, I pondered the truth in my assertion. For all my regrets at what I'd lost, it appeared I'd gained a huge amount too. I needed to remember that. And although Ollie might be impressionable enough to have admired the confident, toppy persona I used to adopt every time I snorted a line of coke, this was the real me, and this was the person he'd fallen for. I just had to hope it was enough to keep him interested.

# Chapter Thirteen

The following night, after he'd demolished a couple of cans of lager in front of a *Star Trek* omnibus, Ollie pulled something out of his satchel.

"Thought you might like this for our evening's entertainment."

"You brought porn?" Every night since I'd returned from hospital, we'd watched one of my DVDs. I might not have been able to get it up, but we had fun laughing at the cheesy lines and contrived situations, and I made sure Ollie always got off, even if I couldn't.

"Yeah. My ex used to have it, and I'd sometimes watch it during the day while he was out. Took it with me when I left. Didn't think he'd miss it."

That was the most Ollie had told me about his previous relationship to date, but I was too distracted by the cover of the DVD to ask more. *Layin' Down with the Law* promised plenty of hot bear/twink action, and the cover showed a young, skinny guy in handcuffs being shafted by a huge, hairy guy in a cop's hat.

"This one of your favourites, then?" I asked.

Ollie held my gaze and gave me a smile I didn't know how to interpret. "Oh, yeah, it's a favourite. Get yourself comfy, and I'll stick it in." He waggled his eyebrows suggestively and leered. The lad clearly couldn't hold his alcohol.

The film turned out to have a certain charm. I might not have been as taken by the burly bear of a cop as Ollie was, but the parade of jailbait criminals needing his particular brand of discipline was appealing. Not nearly as appealing as Ollie, though. I could tell he was excited, watching those boys being bossed around. When the cop ordered one to put his hands against the wall and spread his legs, Ollie gasped. I could see the bulge of his hard-on and wondered why he wasn't yet touching himself. Maybe I should try issuing a few orders.

"Open your jeans and get your dick out," I said, and I didn't even need to try to make my voice sound gruff.

Ollie's eyes were black saucers as he fumbled with his fly, and when he'd released his cock, he put both hands back onto the sofa.

Interesting.

"Stroke yourself. Slowly at first. Yeah, that's it."

A strange sensation started to grow inside me. Fear, excitement, arousal—what was it? All I knew was my heart was hammering wildly, but my body stayed still and calm. I focused on watching Ollie, trying to work out what he needed from me. A sheen of perspiration formed on his brow as he stared at me, the big bad bear on screen forgotten.

I watched his hand moving slow and deliberate, the flushed head of his cock revealed every time he pulled the foreskin down. He looked thoroughly debauched, sitting there fully clothed with just his dick out, waiting for me to tell him what to do.

I wasn't about to start calling him a dirty little ho like the cop on the DVD was with his current victim, and I didn't want to hurt him physically. I'd had more than enough pain in my life, and I certainly wasn't about to inflict it on anyone else. Whips, chains and paddles were all out, not that I owned any in the first place. What did that leave me with? Did he want me to tie him up? The thought made me uncomfortable. Ollie's energetic movement was one of the things that first caught my eye, so the idea of restraining him didn't appeal.

Then I remembered what I had left. What I could still use even though my dick refused to play along and I barely had the energy to lift a finger.

My voice.

My fantasies.

"One of these days, we're going to put this film on again, and I'm going to strip you naked and bend you over the end of that sofa. You'll have to keep your hands on the cushion and spread your legs for me."

Ollie moaned, and he shifted his legs wider apart as if he was already living it in his head.

I felt encouraged to continue. "I'm going to pull your cheeks apart and tease you with my fingers and tongue. I'm going to work your pretty little hole until you're begging me to stick my dick in there. Yeah, that's it, you can speed up now." It was a redundant command, seeing as how he already had, but he seemed to like getting permission if the way he thrust up into his grip was anything to go by. "Use your other hand to cup your balls. That's it. Give them a little squeeze and roll them around."

It was bittersweet, watching Ollie pleasure himself at my command. I wanted to be doing the things I was describing to him. I wanted to sink into him, bury myself in him and pound him hard the way he was clearly craving. I wanted to feel his pulsing heat around me and the ripple of his muscles as he shot his load.

But all I could do for now was give him the imaginary version, so I tried to make it good. "You're going to feel amazing, all tight and hot and needy. I'm going to screw you so long and hard you'll be feeling me for days. It'll be like I'm still inside you, you'll be that well fucked."

Ollie's head thrashed around on the sofa cushion. His eyes were screwed shut, his mouth open, and he looked so beautiful I started choking up.

"I'm not going to let you come until you're so ready for it you're shaking and your cock is leaking everywhere, and then I'm going to take it in my hands and you're going to come so hard you'll feel like your balls have exploded."

Ollie whimpered, and I gathered up enough strength to shift closer to him. I placed my hand on his, amazed to feel how damp he was from all the sweat and precome. He didn't pause in his frenzied rhythm, so I moved my hand and rested it on his thigh instead.

"Shit, Ben, I've got to come." Ollie really did look desperate, his eyes dark and wild.

I kissed him, tasting sweat sharp and salty on his lips. "Do it," I rasped.

I'd never heard anything quite like the sound Ollie made when he came. The raw pleasure was wrapped up with something else, something that touched me deep inside and spread warmth out from that place. As he fell, trembling, into my arms, I knew I was in trouble.

If it felt this good being with him, even without an orgasm, how the hell was I ever going to cope on my own again?

Eventually, Ollie stirred, and I realised the DVD had played itself out at some point while we'd embraced.

"I'd better get going, then...unless you've changed your mind?"

He sounded so hopeful, but I wasn't ready for him to start

staying over. I wasn't ready to let another man sleep beside me. To see me at my most vulnerable.

"My belly's still sore. I don't want you accidentally kneeing me in your sleep."

"I don't mind kipping on the sofa."

I shook my head, steeling myself against those wounded puppy-dog eyes. He leant down to press a kiss to my lips, then stole out quietly. Once Ollie had left, I discovered I didn't even have the energy to get up out of the sofa. I twisted enough so that I was lying down, pulled the throw over me, and thanked my lucky stars I wasn't drinking enough yet to have to go for a piss before bed.

But as I lay there, alone, telling myself it was for the best that I didn't get too attached, I knew I was a lost cause.

I was already head over heels. And I was scared shitless.

Another week passed as my body slowly knitted itself back together again. Zoe hadn't been around as often as she used to be, but that was making things easier for everyone. I didn't need to see her wounded resentment every time she looked at Ollie, and Ollie's resultant confusion. She was trying, I could tell, but it didn't change the way she felt deep down.

I sighed. The midafternoon sun slanted through the blinds in my office, and I couldn't concentrate on the lines of code on my screen.

I needed Ollie. A warm feeling grew inside my belly every time I thought of him. It tingled like my body was about to wake up and shake off all this inertia. I still hadn't had a proper hard-on since the surgery, but right now, thinking about Ollie's ready smile and warm brown eyes, my cock definitely swelled a little. I had another two weeks to go before getting the all-clear for sex, and the idea of an orgasm wrenching thorough my tender insides still made me twitchy, but I was interested in seeing how my body reacted to Ollie's proximity.

Ollie wasn't in the kitchen, sitting at the table poring over his plans like I'd expected. The living room gave off that silent vibe that empty rooms always do, and I was sure I hadn't heard him leave. Where the hell was he?

Then I heard the off-key singing from the bathroom. What was he still doing in there? He'd had a quick shower when he got back from his morning's mission to collect tables and chairs for the café, but I was sure I'd heard him leave the bathroom afterwards. He couldn't still be showering, could he? His hair might take him an age to spike to his satisfaction, but he wasn't that high maintenance. Still, the idea of finding him naked and soapy sent a shiver of anticipation through me, and I pushed the door open, my heart pounding against my rib cage.

The scent of artificial lemons hit me like a bucket of cold water. I found Ollie fully clothed on his knees in the shower stall, scrubbing at the tiles with a scouring pad and what looked like an entire bottle of cream cleaner.

"What are you doing? You don't need to do that!"

Ollie looked up in surprise. "I got hair dye in the grout. It's okay; I don't mind cleaning up my own mess."

"I don't want you to scrub my bathroom." I felt my fists clenching and grabbed hold of the edge of the sink to steady myself. I caught a glimpse of myself in the mirror. I looked really pissed off. I took a deep breath and tried to control the rising anger.

"Ben? You all right, mate?"

The concern in his voice just riled me up even more. "I'm fine! I don't need you checking up on me all the time, and I can do my own housework now." I might be excruciatingly slow and tire myself out after twenty minutes, but I was proud of the fact I'd started pulling my own weight again. "I cleaned the oven this morning."

Ollie frowned and got up to his feet. "Yeah, I know you can look after yourself. It just seemed rude to leave your shower looking like someone had slaughtered an animal in there, and the dye's a bugger to get shifted if you don't clean it straight away."

"Ollie, I want a boyfriend. An equal. I don't want a fucking houseboy twink, okay?"

Something passed over Ollie's face then, and I couldn't understand it. All I knew was that I'd hurt him. But then he gave a strange smile and handed me the scouring pad.

"Right. I'll leave it, then, shall I? Wouldn't want anyone to mistake me for a *houseboy*." His voice was bright—too bright—and he wouldn't meet my eyes. "I've got things to do, anyway. I'll be back later."

"What time should I expect you?"

"Dunno. Might be tomorrow, actually. Things to do. People to see."

"Don't be like that. Come on, Ollie, talk to me."

"Nothing to say right now." Ollie pushed past me and headed to the front door.

I followed, a ringing in my ears sounding a warning signal. What had I said? I replayed my words and groaned.

Ollie had his skateboard in his hand and was pushing open the front door.

"I'm sorry I called you a houseboy twink. I didn't mean it."

But Ollie just shook his head and turned tear-filled eyes in my direction. "I just want some time on my own, okay?" Before I could respond, he was running down the driveway.

"Come back!" I yelled after him. I stumbled after him, collapsing against the dividing wall as Ollie wove his way down the road on that bloody board.

"Shit!" I pounded my fist on the wall, but it didn't improve my mood. The gnome Mrs. F. had placed on the end post grinned at me with a moronic, painted-on smile. I dashed the smug little bastard off there and watched him smash to pieces on the edge of a potted plant.

I still didn't feel any better.

Why couldn't I just accept a good thing when it dropped into my lap? I cursed my stupid pride for not letting him carry on cleaning the damn shower. Would it have hurt me to accept his help graciously, instead of flinging it back in his face?

# Chapter Fourteen

I spent the next forty minutes staring at my mobile but not daring to dial. I'd already screwed things up, and I didn't want to risk saying something else that would cause Ollie pain. And more to the point, I didn't know if he'd want to talk to me.

I was still staring at the display of his number when I heard the rapping on the door. My heart sank. I knew that knock, and I knew I had some explaining to do.

"Mrs. Felpersham. I'm sorry about your gnome."

Mrs. F. peered up at me, but she wasn't on the warpath like I'd expected. No, she seemed far more subdued than I'd seen her before. Worried, perhaps, her face pale and drawn.

"That's not important. You can buy me a new one. Now, Ben, what's going on between you and that young man?"

I really didn't want to bear the brunt of her homophobia again. "I know you don't like him, but you'll have to get used to him. He's my boyfriend."

She pierced me with a sharp gaze. "Whatever makes you think I don't like him?"

"You lost him his job!"

"What are you talking about?" Mrs. F. genuinely looked puzzled, and my previous certainty about the identity of the mysterious busybody who'd grassed up Ollie started to crumble.

"Someone reported him to his boss for fraternising with the customers. I thought it must have been you. And you didn't pass on that message when I was in hospital."

Mrs. F. stared at me for a long minute, and I wanted to hide. Finally, she spoke. "I'm going to ignore that first remark and suggest you get your facts straight." I coloured, remembering using those exact words to her when she accused Ollie of messing up her gnome delivery. "I apologise for not being here to pass on the note, but I was called to visit my sister who'd been very sick. It certainly wasn't deliberate."

"Oh, I, er... Sorry. Is she okay?"

Mrs. F. sniffed and looked away. That was the moment when I noticed she was dressed entirely in black. Somehow I didn't think she'd suddenly decided to become a goth.

"Oh shit. I mean, Christ, I'm sorry. That's rough."

"It happens to us all in the end, though, doesn't it? The only certainties in life are death and taxes." Mrs. F. gave a wry laugh. "She told me something on her deathbed, though. She said her only regret was not encouraging her stubborn idiot of a sister to run after the man she loved."

"Her sister? Oh, right." I studied Mrs. F., and for the first time, I saw not an interfering, old battle-axe but a lonely spinster, pining for the love she had lost. I realised I was staring when Mrs. F. fixed me with her shrewd gaze.

"Ben, he might be young and look like a reprobate, but he's a good lad. Always smiling, always waves hello to me. If you love him, go after him. Life's too short to waste it being angry."

I wondered how much of our doorstep argument she'd seen and heard. But I wasn't going to waste time being embarrassed. She was right. I'd been a tosser, and I needed to put things right.

"Thanks, Mrs. F." I swept her up in a hug and kissed her lavishly on the cheek.

"Well, I never!" she exclaimed as I set her back down again. She patted her hair as if I'd messed it up, but I didn't miss the smile that twitched at her lips.

I grabbed my mobile from the kitchen table and dialled. There was no point trying to find him if he didn't want to be found. When he picked up on the third ring, my breath shuddered out of me.

"Ollie, I'm sorry I screwed up."

"It's okay." Ollie sniffed as if he'd been crying, but his voice was level. "I was being a right drama queen, wasn't I? Surprised you're not sick of me already."

"Don't be ridiculous. I just... I overreacted. I shouldn't have been so bloody touchy."

"Nah, don't worry about it. It was me, not you."

"Could I come and see you? Talk about it in person? I don't want you being upset on your own."

"It's cool, Ben. I'm having a cup of tea with Meera, and I've got a shift at the café this evening. Don't blow it out of proportion, yeah? I'm fine."

As he sounded more upbeat and positive than when he'd answered, I decided to take the opt out he'd offered. "Will I see you in the morning, then?"

"Try keeping me away," he teased. "I'll miss you tonight."

"Yeah, me too."

"Laters."

When I hung up, the relief poured through me like soothing balm. It was scary, needing him this badly. Scary when it appeared I could fuck it up just by opening my mouth.

The next day, Ollie arrived on my doorstep with a smile and a kiss, and it was easy to gloss over the previous day by ignoring it and getting down to business. My version of business for the morning being Ollie's dick having an appointment in my mouth. I ambushed him before he'd had a chance to put his bag down and pushed him against the hallway wall.

"Mornin', Ben. Good to see you too." Ollie's chuckle did funny things to my insides. I claimed his mouth with my own before I could say anything stupid. I wasn't going to scare him off with my howling pit of need.

I fumbled his trousers open, sank to my knees and swallowed him down like he was all my forbidden foods wrapped up in one meaty package. Ollie tasted so fucking sweet I wanted to devour him. I slid my fingers back towards his hole, wondering what he'd taste like there. I'd have to try that soon, somewhere more comfy. The idea sent a hot pulse of blood to my dick. My knees groaned on the hard floor, but I couldn't deny the fact that my dick had finally woken up and taken a proper interest in proceedings. I tried my best to ignore it and concentrated on working Ollie's hole with my fingers as I mouthed the end of his cock. I fluttered my fingertips just inside him, and he made a strangled noise. I could feel his muscles working to pull me in, could sense his dilemma as he had to choose whether to push farther into my mouth or back onto my fingers.

He thrust back, his hot heat enveloping me. God, it was going to feel so good to sink my cock into him and fuck him properly. I swept over his gland and swallowed him down, loving the way he attempted to grab hold of my cropped hair as he came. It took my mind off the party in my pants, and I could fool myself that I wasn't really all that excited. That it was just a pale imitation of Ollie's pleasure.

But I hadn't fooled Ollie.

"Are you going to let me do something about that now?" he asked, a whine creeping into his voice. "Please, Ben. Let me take care of you. It should be fine now the stitches are out, shouldn't it?"

I'd been using them as an excuse, I realised, but I wasn't about to admit to having performance anxiety, and I still had the doctor to back me up. "You know I'm supposed to wait another fortnight. Come on, Ollie, give me a break. I don't want to mess this all up just because I'm feeling horny."

He pouted. "Don't see how a hand job could do any harm. It's not like you'd have to move much. No more than you have been every day now you're exercising again. Makes me think you just don't want me to."

"You know that's rubbish. Just... God, just give me another couple of weeks, okay?"

I kissed him to prevent him replying, and when we parted he headed to the kitchen table without a word.

In the hallway that night, on his way out, he gave me another drawing. In it I was lying back on a bed, and he was kneeling between my legs, sucking me off, his arse thrust high in brazen invitation, his hole gaping. I groaned.

"You like it?" Ollie asked, his cheeks dimpling in mischief.

"I... Of course I like it! I just—"

"Let me, Ben. Please? I need to do something for you." His hand snaked down to my crotch, and I slapped it away, annoyed.

"Why?" I demanded, and the way he flinched made me even more irritated. "Why are you so desperate to get me off? Can't you just enjoy what I'm giving you and leave it at that? Jesus, how much more do you need? I'm doing everything I can!"

His lips twisted into something like a smile but which looked wrong. "I didn't realise it was such a chore," he said bitterly.

"It's not a fucking chore!" I shouted.

He looked ready to bolt, and I grabbed hold of his arms, ashamed to see the fear in his eyes. Shit, had I put that there? I loosened my grip, kneading with my fingers in what I hoped was a reassuring manner. "Look, I don't know how to put this in a way that will make sense, but spending time with you has been brilliant, and all I want right now is to treat you well. You aren't obliged to give me anything back." *You've already given me more than you'll ever know,* I wanted to add but couldn't force the words out.

He stared back at me, his eyes wide and uncomprehending.

"But I should. I feel guilty always taking. You're older and bigger, and you're the top, so I should be servicing you."

"Who told you that bullshit?" I really was angry now. "That's not the way it works, Ollie. People are too bloody complicated to be put in little boxes like that. If you want someone to boss you around, if you get a kick out of being used, then you're with the wrong guy."

Ollie's gaze dropped. "I'm sorry," he murmured. "I fucked up, didn't I?"

"No, you didn't. You just have a screwy idea of how relationships work. This ex of yours, is that how he wanted things?"

"I don't wanna talk about him." Ollie's lips were tight, so I didn't quiz him any further.

"Okay, just remember, this is our relationship, and we make our own rules. We don't have to follow anyone else's."

Ollie nodded, smiled and kissed me goodnight as usual. I

watched him start up Rogue and pull away into the night with a mix of relief and regret. I hoped I'd said the right things to him, but it was hard to know what his problem was if he wouldn't talk to me about it.

I lay awake for a long time, running through scenarios in my head, each more alarming than the last. In the end, I told myself I might never know what this ex had done to him, and succumbed to an uneasy sleep.

# Chapter Fifteen

"What's this?" Zoe's voice was muffled by the refrigerator, but I could hear the chill of disapproval.

"What's what?" I asked, slowly swirling the hot water over a dirty plate. I might not have been fast at household chores, but I was deriving a strange sort of enjoyment out of getting back to them again.

"This." Zoe lifted out a small plastic container of orange mush. "I didn't make this for you. Has he started cooking for you now as well?" Her tone was resentful, but I could hear the tremor of tears underneath it.

"Zo, you're overreacting."

"I'm not! I'm fucking well being replaced, and you don't need me anymore. How the hell am I supposed to react to that?"

"Jesus Christ!" I dropped the plate into the sink and heard something crack. Didn't matter. My little sister was hurting.

I grasped her around the shoulders, but she turned her head away, glowering at the wall. "Look at me. Zoe, come on! That's better. Now listen carefully, because this is the truth. You are not being replaced. No one could ever replace you, because you're my sister and I love you with all my heart."

"How can you?" she wailed.

I shook my head, baffled. "How can I what? Love you?"

"You can't love me with all your heart when you love him too."

"That's not how love works. It doesn't diminish when you love more people. It grows. There isn't a finite amount of it, you know." She was giving me that "yeah, right" look she does so well, so I cast my mind around for an example to prove what I was saying. "I didn't love Mum and Dad any less when you came along. I thought I would. To begin with, I resented you for taking away their attention. Everything was 'baby this' and 'Zoe that' for a while."

Zoe sniffled but lifted her watery eyes to mine. "What changed?"

"Nothing, really. Just me. I realised you weren't going to go away, so I decided I may as well try to get along with you. Then I noticed how cute you were, and before I knew it, I was reading you picture books and throwing you in the air to make you giggle."

"Are you saying I should try throwing Ollie around?"

I made a face like I was seriously contemplating it. "You could try tickling him. He's pretty ticklish behind the ears."

Zoe gave a tremulous smile. "I'll try."

"That would be good, because he's not going anywhere and it would make me so happy if the two of you could get along. He's a really nice bloke, Zo."

"I know. I know he is, really. I just get so wound up when I see things like this." She gestured in the direction of the tub that had started the whole episode. "That's my job. I love cooking for you."

"No one's trying to replace you, little sis." I kissed the top of her head. "And if you'd waited for a moment before going off on a wobbler, you'd have found out that isn't for me. It's one of Ollie's experimental organic baby food recipes for the café."

Zoe giggled and wiped her nose on her sleeve. “I’ve been a right idiot, haven’t I?”

“No comment.”

“Is it any good? The baby food?”

“Try it and see.”

Zoe grabbed a teaspoon from the washing up and sampled a tentative mouthful. “Not bad. Could do with a little garlic, though.”

“You can’t feed babies garlic.”

“Who says? You’d be surprised. Hmmm...” Zoe took another mouthful, then another. “This is good, though. D’you think Ollie would mind if I gave him some tips?”

I considered it. Would Ollie think she was sticking her nose in? Given what I knew of Ollie, I thought not. He wouldn’t even agree that Mrs. F. was an interfering old biddy and had given her the benefit of the doubt over the whole letter thing. “I think it would be a great idea. He’d love some advice from someone with your culinary expertise.”

“Cool.” Zoe smiled, and this time, she genuinely looked happy.

I decided I’d have to work on making sure she felt appreciated. “How about I take you out to dinner at the weekend? Sunday lunch at the Little Angel?” It was a place on the river in Henley, and Zoe had always loved eating there as a kid. I used to tell her she was my Little Angel and they’d named the place after her. It had gone a bit gastropub these days, but the grown-up Zoe would probably appreciate the enhanced menu with added marinated unpronounceables and sun-dried whatevers.

“Sunday? Won’t Ollie be working then?”

“Yes, but I’m asking you. Just you and me, out for a meal

like old times. What do you say?"

Zoe hugged me tight. "Can we feed the ducks afterwards?"

I grinned. "Those greedy little bastards? Of course we can."

My kitchen had turned into some kind of baby-food research lab. Zoe and Ollie dodged around each other in a crazy dance as they grabbed ingredients, jotted down notes and stuck their fingers into bowls of goop, pulling faces that ranged from disgust to delight as they sampled the flavours. I watched from my seat at the kitchen table, bemused by the whirlwind of activity.

Every now and then, Ollie would shoot me a look that communicated just how grateful he was for me talking things through with Zoe. Then Zoe would shout out an order or smack him on the bum, and he'd roll his eyes at me.

But eventually, they were ready. Ollie placed the twelve pots of mush in front of me with a flourish. Each contained a wooden lolly stick with a different letter written on the end, and a teaspoon. Oh goodie.

"Do I have to?" I pleaded.

"Don't be such a baby," Zoe said. "You're our chief taster."

"I thought being a baby was the whole point," I grumbled, but I lifted the spoon in the nearest pot and had a sniff before tasting. It was yellow and smelled faintly spicy. I opened my mouth and hoped for the best.

It was sweet. So sweet my taste buds went into overdrive. "Are you sure this is okay for me to eat?"

"It's all fine," Ollie reassured me. "No added salt or sugar, no e-numbers, no artificial colours or preservatives. Just fruit, vegetables and cereals."

"It tastes like curry. Can babies eat curry?"

"Yes!" they exclaimed in unison, giving each other a look of exasperated affection.

I decided to shut up in case they ganged up on me again and took another mouthful. It was surprisingly good, actually. I decided I needed one more to make a proper assessment.

Ollie whipped the bowl away. "Don't fill yourself up with the first one. You've got eleven more to go."

"So, how would you rate sample A for appearance, texture, aroma and flavour?" Zoe asked, clipboard in hand. "I want marks out of ten for each."

I groaned, but I did my best to answer for each different sample. There were a couple that weren't to my taste, including one made with ginger and parsnip, but on the whole, I was really impressed. The blueberry-and-apricot one was particularly good, we all agreed.

"You know, you could get some moulds and make this one into ice-lollies," Zoe suggested after taking another spoonful. "It would be much cheaper than buying them in, and it could be a unique selling point for you."

"That's a brilliant idea!" Ollie beamed at Zoe.

"I'm full of them," Zoe said. Modesty had never been one of her strong points, particularly when her cooking was involved.

"What she's not telling you is about the time she had a brilliant idea to make jacket potatoes with banana and beetroot mashed inside."

"Hey! I liked them," Zoe protested.

"You only said that to save face. I could see the way you grimaced every time you swallowed. Potatoes shouldn't be pink, and they shouldn't taste of banana."

"This man is the antithesis of Heston Blumenthal, Ollie. I

hope you realise that. He wouldn't recognise innovative cuisine if you poked him in the eye with it. We had pasta or fish and chips every single night before I took over the cooking."

"Yeah, and then we had takeaway pizza every other night because you'd made something so gross even you wouldn't eat it."

Zoe had her hands on her hips, squaring off at me. "I was ten years old and entirely self-taught. Give me a break!"

"All I'm saying is maybe you should have started with simple stuff rather than diving straight in with the gourmet recipes."

"But they looked so much prettier!"

"Pretty isn't the same as tasty."

Ollie's gaze moved between the two of us, clearly amused at the squabbling, but I thought I saw something else in his expression too, so I reined it back in and changed the subject.

Later, once Zoe had left and we were working our way through the pile of dirty dishes, I asked Ollie if everything was okay.

"Yeah, of course. Why d'you ask?"

"I thought you looked a bit put out when me and Zo were arguing. You know it's only for fun, don't you?"

"Oh yeah. I get that. I just...I guess I felt a bit sad, that's all."

"Sad? What for?" I handed Ollie a dripping saucepan, and he began to dry it, but then set it down on the worktop.

"Just that me and my brother are probably never gonna have a relationship like you and Zoe have. I mean, I never really get to see him these days."

"Why not? Things aren't that bad between you and your stepdad, are they?"

Ollie heaved a sigh. then looked me straight in the eyes. "It's not that they won't let me visit or anything. I just feel so awkward there, like a spare part. They're all so close, doesn't feel like there's any room for me."

I thought about it for a moment as I washed goop off the teaspoons. I didn't want to interfere in Ollie's life, but then again, maybe he wanted a bit of direction. He had seemed to like it whenever I'd taken charge of things.

"We'll go and see them together," I announced. "As soon as I'm feeling fit again. That way you'll feel like you belong with me, so it won't be awkward."

Ollie stared down at his saucepan and didn't reply, and I wondered if I was presuming too much. "That's if you want me to, anyway. It's your call."

"Of course I want you there! Would you really want to meet them?"

Ollie's eyes gleamed so bright with emotion I was alarmed, but I reassured him as best I could that I really did want to know his family.

But as we sat and watched an old episode of *Babylon Five* later that evening, our conversation played through my head again. It was sobering to realise just how dependent Ollie was on me, and how willingly he deferred to what I wanted. I had a huge responsibility towards his happiness, I realised, and I really couldn't bear the idea of screwing it up in any way.

I'd have to be extremely careful how I exercised the power Ollie had given to me.

# Chapter Sixteen

As my body healed from the surgery, I experienced a surge of energy like I hadn't had in years, so when James suggested I might like to come into the office for a meeting with clients and to see the old team again, I readily agreed. It had been only eighteen days since leaving hospital, but I was ready to see a bit more of the world than the walls of my flat and the outpatients' clinic.

"Can I come with you?" Ollie asked as I stood in front of the mirror, checking the fit of my suit. Now that I wasn't bloated with dialysate anymore, I could get back into my old clothes again. In fact, if anything, they were a little baggy around the waist. I tightened my belt another notch.

"Are you sure you want to? It'll be pretty boring. I'll be in a meeting for most of the time."

"I want to see where you used to work."

I'd come to recognise that determined set of Ollie's jaw, so I smiled affably and agreed. God knew what James and the others would make of him and his bright red hair, but it wasn't exactly a secret that I was gay, so they'd just have to deal with it.

"How do I look?" I asked Ollie. "Can you see the tube through these?" I'd stuck the thing down with double the amount of tape I usually used, but it still made me paranoid, especially wearing trousers that clung very differently from the jeans I'd been favouring since leaving hospital. At least I didn't have as much resentment of my tube as I used to, though. Now it wasn't being used and I knew its days were numbered, I could put up with it with much better grace.

Ollie's hands dropped onto my shoulders, massaging me through the layers of shirt and jacket. "With shoulders like these, no one's going to be looking anywhere else."

"You like my shoulders?" This was news to me.

"Your shoulders are bloody awesome. Really broad and strong looking."

I raised my eyebrows at my reflection. Okay, maybe I could see what Ollie was getting at. It was an expensive jacket with a flattering cut, after all. I grinned at Ollie in the mirror.

"Go get 'em, Tiger," he teased.

We headed on out, and when I used my remote to open the garage door, Ollie's eyes just about popped out of his head. "We're taking the MG?"

"It is my car."

"You sure you'll be up for driving on the way back?"

"I'll be fine." I bit back the annoyance at being mollycoddled. He had a valid point, much as I didn't like to hear it. I might be feeling better than I had been, but I was still a long way from recovered. "If I'm not, then you can drive us."

"Me? You'd let me? Really?" Ollie was practically dancing on the spot.

I rolled my eyes. "Only as a last resort. Come on, behave yourself."

Ollie batted his eyelashes at me. "Did I tell you yet how sexy you look in that suit?"

"Flattery will get you many places but not behind the wheel

of my car."

"Spoilsport." Ollie pouted, but his eyes still gleamed with pleasure.

"Climb on in. You're making me feel tired just watching you jump around."

Ollie was suitably impressed by the journey to the office, running his hands over the walnut dashboard and singing the praises of the leather interior. I turned the heated seats on just to amuse him, even though the weather was mild. When we pulled up outside the office, he was positively awestruck.

"Swanky," he breathed.

I glanced out at the imposing stone facade, impeccably manicured topiary and gleaming brass plate by the door. "You get used to it."

His face fell.

"All right. I admit it, it's swanky." I turned to see what Ollie was staring at and saw James walking down the street with a man who could only be Dane Gibson, the client I was here to meet. There was the same manicured goatee and smug smile I remembered from the photograph on his website. "I'd better get going. That's my boss over there. Are you coming?" I asked as I opened my door.

Ollie hunched down into the seat like he was trying to make himself as small as possible. "I think I'll wait out here."

He wasn't feeling intimidated by the place, was he?

"You'd be very welcome. Tamara'll make you coffee and treat you to all her kids' life histories while you wait. She's got whole albums of baby photos tucked under her desk." Most blokes would run a mile, but Ollie would probably enjoy that sort of thing.

"Nah, I'm fine."

Ollie didn't sound fine, but as I was running a little late already, I told myself I'd get to the bottom of it after my meeting. I wanted to kiss him goodbye, but I wasn't used to public displays of affection, so I settled for a quick ruffle of his hair instead. "Okay. I'll leave you the keys in case you want to stretch your legs, but don't you dare drive off anywhere."

"Don't worry, I won't," Ollie mumbled.

I shook my head as I crossed the street. I couldn't spare the time to try to figure out this latest mood swing. Must be one of his drama-queen moments again. My attention shaped itself around the notes I'd made in preparation for meeting the client, but I did remember to turn and wave before heading into the lobby.

Ollie wasn't even looking my way.

"Right. I think that just about wraps everything up for the moment." James shuffled his notes and fixed us all with a beady gaze. "Do you all have everything you need?"

I glanced down at my own notes and nodded my assent. Dane Gibson might be a little self-satisfied for my liking, but he clearly had reason to be. His feedback to the team on our work so far had been succinct, constructive and challenging without being overtly demanding. I could see why his company was such a success with him at the helm.

"Ben, could I have a quick word?" Dane asked as I rose to leave.

Puzzled, I stopped in my tracks. If there was a problem with my work, I couldn't understand why he hadn't brought it up earlier.

Dane waited for the others to leave the office, promising

James he'd be out in a moment. I stood there, trying to calm my nerves and surreptitiously wipe my sweaty palms on my jacket. But then Dane stepped close. Too close. We were of a height, and his piercing blue eyes stared right into mine. A smile curved his lips—one that made my heart beat faster.

"I can see you're my kind of man," Dane said, his voice dripping with suggestion. "I'd like to meet up for a drink later. Get to know each other better."

I swallowed hard. My gaydar might be rusty, but it was impossible to miss the subtext with him right up close and personal. "I appreciate the offer, but I don't think my boyfriend would be too happy about that."

"Pity." He gave me a long look up and down. I wanted to hide behind the nearest filing cabinet, but he seemed to like what he saw, if the look on his face was anything to go by. He handed me a card. "If you change your mind sometime and want to take me up on the offer, just get in touch."

I politely promised I would and took the card. It wouldn't do to upset one of our top clients now, would it? Dane gave me one last lecherous grin and sauntered out to find James.

Five minutes later, I'd taken leave of everyone in the office, fielding all their kind words and offers of help with as much grace as I could manage, but I was too tired to hang around for long, and I desperately wanted to get home again. The thought of Ollie waiting for me in the car was a real comfort, and I headed out as fast as I could.

Ollie wasn't there.

I crossed the street, worry and irritation wrestling inside me. As I pulled out my mobile to give him a call, I looked in the driver's side window and saw him huddled up on the seat, like he was trying to take up as little space as possible. Was he sleeping? I tried the door, but it was locked.

I knocked on the window, and Ollie startled, whipping his head around with a panicked expression. It melted into relief as he caught sight of me. He reached up to unlock the door and slid across into his own seat.

"You okay?" I asked. "Thought I was the only one of us who needed naps during the day."

"Yeah, fine. How'd it go?"

He didn't exactly sound or look fine, but I took his words at face value for the time being as I wanted to get home and comfortable before beginning a draining discussion.

"It was good. A little tiring, perhaps." I started the engine and was pulling out into traffic when I continued. "Our new client knows exactly how he wants things, which is great in some ways, but means we can't cut any corners. I'll be busy these next few weeks."

Ollie mumbled something, and I couldn't pick out the words, but he sounded grumpy.

I tried to cheer him up. "The guy's such an overconfident prick he even tried to ask me out. Can you believe it? His gaydar must be a lot better than mine, or maybe he just tries it on with every guy he meets."

Ollie didn't answer. I risked a quick glance over at him on a straight stretch of road. His face was like thunder. God, he wasn't the jealous type, was he?

"I turned him down, you'll be pleased to know."

"Dane asked you out?" Ollie asked, like he hadn't even heard anything I'd said since.

"Yeah, I know. I'm as surprised as you are. It's okay, though. I'm not interested in him."

"I can't believe Dane asked you out." Ollie's tone was flat—I couldn't remember ever hearing him speak that way before.

Was he feeling pissed off and left out because I was getting back to the life I'd had before the kidney failure? Before I'd ever met him?

I negotiated a tricky junction in silence, and then it dawned on me. I'd never mentioned Dane's name to Ollie, had I? I glanced over again and was stunned to see tears in his eyes.

I kept my voice calm and reassuring, despite my nerves thrumming and my heart jittering. "Whatever it is you're not telling me, we need to have a talk about it when we get back."

Ollie nodded, sniffed, and a tear ran down his cheek.

I attempted to keep my mind blank as I drove back across Reading. There was no point indulging in useless speculation when I didn't have any facts. Dane could be anything to Ollie. Just because he was gay didn't mean they'd had a relationship of any kind. Of course, by the time we'd pulled into my driveway, I was bursting with possible scenarios.

Ollie remained seated as I got out of the car. He hadn't even undone his seat belt. The silent tears had stopped falling, thank God, but he looked dazed. I opened his door and spoke softly to him.

"Come on inside. Whatever it is, you'll feel better when you've shared it." I wasn't convinced of that myself, but it's what I always used to say to Zoe whenever she came home from school in tears.

Ollie nodded and followed me into the house, his movements stiff and his arms wrapped tight around himself. I led him to the kitchen and set about making tea. My body was exhausted, and I was dimly aware that I'd be paying for overdoing it soon enough, but the adrenaline seemed to be keeping me going for the moment.

I sat down opposite him and watched him cradle the cup in his hands, staring down into it as if he expected to find the answers there. Although what the question was, I wasn't entirely sure just yet.

"Are you ready to talk?"

"I think so."

I waited a long time, and finally the words began, so low I had to strain to hear them.

"He's my ex. Dane, I mean. We were together…a long time. Four years."

"Four years? You're only twenty now."

Ollie nodded miserably. "Since I was fifteen," he whispered.

"That's sick." The words were out of my mouth before I'd had time to think, but I regretted them instantly.

"What's sick?" Ollie retaliated, his eyes flashing. "Being in love with someone older? Thanks a lot."

"But he was an arsehole, taking advantage of your innocence."

"Innocence?" Ollie gave a twisted smile. "You think I'm innocent?"

"You know what I mean. You're young. You're too trusting. You wear your heart on your sleeve. You could easily be used by someone older and more experienced. Made to do things you weren't ready for." I wished I could shut up as I watched the expression on Ollie's face grow darker and darker. "You've got this urge to look after people that could easily be exploited by someone clever."

"You think I'm just a doormat, don't you?" Ollie rose and glared at me. "I don't need to listen to this right now."

He stormed out the door, and I followed as fast as I could, although my legs seemed to have lost all coordination and my mind was spinning.

"Wait, Ollie, just listen to me." I reached out to stop him opening the front door.

Ollie pushed me back, surprisingly strong in the heat of his anger. I stumbled against the wall and watched him pick up his satchel and board.

"You're overreacting. That's not what I meant."

"I know what you meant. I'm just a stupid kid who doesn't have a proper job and used to be a houseboy." He gave his skateboard a tight smile. "I'm not grown up enough for you."

Ollie used to be Dane's houseboy? My brain scrambled to process that new bit of information as Ollie opened the front door. "Wait, we need to talk. Ollie, please!"

He turned to give me one last look, and this time I saw the tears streaming down his cheeks. "I need some time by myself."

# Chapter Seventeen

I was too tired to do anything like chase after him in the car. The state I was in, I'd have been unsafe on the roads. That's what I told myself as I went to crash out on my sofa, anyway. Underneath it all there was a poisonous little voice in my ear, whispering I'd been taken for a ride. I lay there and gave it time to fill my head with suspicions until I must have drifted off.

"Hey, Benj, you all right?" Zoe's voice roused me from my slumber.

"Huh?" I rubbed my eyes, and the memory of Ollie storming off rose to the top of my consciousness. "Shit!"

"Everything okay? I've been calling you and Ollie, but no one was answering. How'd it go at the meeting?"

I looked up at Zoe. Her face was in shadow, and I realised from the light levels I must have been asleep for some time. "Yeah, the meeting was good. What's the time?"

"Half seven. Where's Ollie got to? I thought he was supposed to be with you this evening. We'd arranged to talk through some café stuff together. He needs tips on dealing with wholesalers, or they'll see him coming a mile off."

"Ollie went out," I snapped.

"What's going on?" Zoe stood over me, her arms folded, and

I knew I wouldn't get away with pretending not to know what she was talking about.

"We had a fight."

"Okay, mind telling me why? Ollie's about the least confrontational person I've ever met."

"Are you accusing me of starting it?"

Zoe just looked at me, her eyebrows disappearing up under her fringe.

"Fine, fine, it was me, okay?"

"No, it's not okay. Why are you picking fights with Ollie?"

"I just found out some stuff about his past. Stuff he should have told me before. You know he used to be a houseboy for this hotshot businessman? Can you see a pattern there?"

"Pattern?"

"Yeah, like he wanted another sugar daddy to replace Dane, and then along came me. You said it yourself, didn't you? You warned me Ollie was a gold-digger."

"Jesus Christ, Benjamin Lethbridge! I cannot believe I'm hearing this crap!"

I sat there, stunned, as Zoe laid into me.

"You don't honestly believe that, do you?"

"Well, it seemed—"

"Has Ollie ever *asked* you for money?"

"No, but—"

"Has he ever asked if he could move in here?"

"No, he hasn't—"

"Has he ever even hinted that he wants something, or given you any real reason to believe that he's in this because of your money?"

I thought long and hard. Zoe was scary when she was

angry. “Um, now that you come to mention it, he’s never really asked me for anything.” Except for the chance to look after me, to do things for me, to make me come. “God, I’ve really fucked things up, haven’t I?”

Zoe plonked herself down onto the sofa next to me. “Listen, Benj, Ollie told me about Dane and the way things were between them, and I can honestly say I don’t think he wants a repeat of that relationship ever again. The things that draw him to you are completely different to the things he fell for about Dane, and even then, I don’t think he was in it for the money.”

“How come he told you and not me?”

“I dunno. Because I actually listen rather than making assumptions, perhaps?”

I probably deserved that, so I swallowed the surge of irritation. “So why was Ollie with Dane?”

“I think you should ask him that yourself, but for what it’s worth, I think Ollie needs someone to look up to. You know he worships the ground you walk on, don’t you? He thinks you bloody well hung the moon. I’m surprised he hasn’t set up some kind of shrine to you. I’ve tried to warn him you’re only human, but to him, you’re some kind of superhero.”

“I’m not worthy of being adored.”

“Well, I know that better than anyone, but I love you anyway.”

“Cheers, Sis,” I grumbled.

“Don’t mention it,” Zoe deadpanned. “You need to be telling Ollie this instead of me. Explain how you feel about it all, yeah?”

“Doesn’t sound like you’re giving me much of a choice.”

She grinned, but I could see the steel in her eyes and the set of her jaw. “I’m not letting you bollocks this up, Benj. I don’t care how young and penniless he is, if he makes you happy."

I nodded. "He does. Okay, I'll do it."

I picked up my mobile and tried his number, but his phone was switched off.

"Where could he be?" Zoe asked. "You must have an idea."

"I'll have to try his mate Omar's place."

"Want me to come with you?"

"Thanks, but I should do this on my own." I pulled Zoe into a fierce hug. "You're the best, you know that?"

Zoe squeezed me back just as tightly. "You too. Now go get your man."

Ollie had told me he lived above the corner shop on Henley Road, so his address wasn't too difficult to find. Night was already falling as I pulled up in the tiny parking area around the back of the shop, and I had a moment's fear for the safety of the MG there. It might only be a mile from my own place, but it was like another world here, complete with roaming packs of youths in hooded tops out looking for kicks. Still, the car was just a thing; if it got stolen, it got stolen. I wasn't about to let Ollie go because I valued an object more than him.

The flat was accessed by set of metal stairs leading to a balcony around the back, which looked down over the cracked parking area and the overflowing bins. Someone had gone to an effort to cheer up the balcony with a few pots of tulips and pansies, but I could see why Ollie was so impressed with my place on its gentrified street of Victorian semis, all with their own front gardens.

I knocked on the door, and it opened with a waft of sweet incense. A tall, dark-skinned bloke stood backlit by the hallway lighting—the same one I'd seen Ollie with that time I went spying at the ramps. It could only be Omar. He was wearing nothing more than a pair of baggy silk trousers and a ferocious scowl. With his shaved head and hooked nose, he looked like some kind of warrior out of the Arabian Nights.

"He's not here," Omar announced. He moved to slam the door in my face, but I'd wedged my foot in there. "And you've got some serious grovelling to do, *mate*."

"Wait, how do you know who I am?"

Omar rolled his eyes. "Ollie only goes and shows me the new photos of you on his phone every fucking evening. Then me and Meera get treated to all the latest news about how wonderful you are. It's all 'Ben said this', and 'Ben did that'. Makes me wanna chuck. He's worse with you than he was with Dane."

"Dane?" Did I really want to hear this?

"His ex. Total wanker, that bloke was, but Ollie thought the sun shone out of his arse." Omar's lip curled derisively. "Thought you was gonna treat him better, but you're all the same, aren't you? You older guys who go after the young ones."

"Hey, wait a minute, I don't think you know what's going on here."

"I know enough." Omar shoved the door fully open and took a step forward out onto the balcony, seemingly heedless of the cool evening air on all that naked skin. "I know Ollie came home in a right fucking state because of something you did to him."

Omar was ripped, and I was acutely aware of how easily he could turn me into mincemeat, should he take a dislike to me. Something he already appeared to have done. I backed away from him and nearly crushed a tub of flowers as I stumbled back against the balcony railing. It gave me support, but I still felt horribly vulnerable there, knowing there was a ten-foot drop onto solid concrete right behind me.

"I didn't *do* anything, and I didn't mean to upset him. Is he in there? Please, I need to talk to him."

"Yeah, well, he doesn't need to talk to you, all right? So I suggest you clear off and go fu—"

"Omar Mohammed Khan, you mind your language and get back in here!"

Omar turned at the interruption, and I saw a petite woman at the door to the flat. I say petite because she was tiny compared to Omar, but she had a belly like a beach ball under her hot pink salwar kameez.

Omar made a heated reply in what sounded like Punjabi to my ears, which had been attuned by growing up in an area with a large Pakistani population. Meera gave as good as she got, though, jabbing away with her fingers to emphasise her point. Her gold nose stud twinkled as she shook her head rapidly. Eventually, Omar heaved a sigh and turned to loom over me.

"You better treat him right, hear me? Or I'll come round and break your fucking legs."

"I will. I promise." I tried to make myself look as small as possible, but as he was only an inch or two taller than me, it was tricky.

Omar sniffed contemptuously but obviously considered his masculinity to be appeased enough to strut back into the flat. Meera studied me from the open doorway, her hands resting on top of her belly.

"You must be Ben. It's good to meet you at last. You'll have to come round for dinner sometime soon, once you're allowed to eat normal food again."

"I, uh, thank you. I'm not sure your husband would agree to that."

Meera flapped her hand dismissively. “He'll be fine. His bark's worse than his bite. You sort things out with Ollie, and he'll be happy. Those two've been best mates since they were little children, you know? Omar's always been like a big brother, protecting him from bullies and all that.”

“Ah, I see.”

“Yes. Quite.” It was interesting that despite the fluent Punjabi, Meera had barely a trace of an Asian accent when speaking English. She must have grown up around here. Mind you, the very fact that she wasn't wearing a headscarf and was standing on the doorstep speaking to a strange man suggested she wasn't a first-generation immigrant.

Meera smiled at me as if waiting for me to continue.

“Could I speak to Ollie, please?” I was surprised he hadn't come out of the flat with all the commotion. Maybe he really didn't want to see me. I gulped, trying to keep the desolation at bay. I could still fix this, couldn't I?

“He went out about an hour ago with his skateboard. I expect he'll be at the ramps.”

I looked up at the sky doubtfully. “It's too dark to skate.”

“Yes, well, he likes to hang out down there. He has his coffee shop, of course.”

“Ah, okay.” I turned to leave. “Thanks, Meera.”

“Wait a minute!”

I turned back with a sigh. Here came the warning about not messing Ollie around again. Seemed like everyone I met wanted to give me one of those, like Ollie was some fragile little flower that needed protecting. I could see there was that side to him, but he had a tough streak too. He'd needed it, being out and proud in a neighbourhood like this. Still, I was glad there were so many people out there who had his back.

"When are you going to make an honest man of him?"

"Uh, what?" She wasn't suggesting I propose, was she?

"You know, ask him to move in with you rather than sending him back here every night."

That took me by surprise. "Move in?"

"Yes. I want my privacy back. He needs to be out by the time the baby comes." She stroked her belly possessively. "You've got six weeks."

"Oh. I'll see what I can do."

Meera nodded, completely self-assured. "Yes, Ollie says you're a good man. You'll do right by him."

I wished I had her confidence in myself.

# Chapter Eighteen

The park was gloomy, and for an awful moment, I thought all the gates had been locked, but that was only the first set I tried leading into the small children's play area. I could just make out an open gate near the ramps, so I headed around the perimeter fence and walked in over the damp grass. There was a figure sitting on the base of the nearest ramp. I'd have recognised that spiky-haired silhouette anywhere.

Ollie looked up at me with dark eyes, his expression guarded. It pained me to see him wary, and I crouched down to be at his level.

"Hey," I said softly.

"Hey, yourself." Ollie gave a weak smile, but only his lips seemed to be cooperating.

"Ollie, I'm sorry. I don't know quite what it was I said that screwed everything up, but I think we need to talk about it if we're going to sort it out."

Ollie looked more hopeful at that. "D'you think we can?"

"I hope we can. I just need you to tell me why you ran off like that so I know what to avoid doing in future." I needed him to tell me quickly as well, because crouching like this was hell on my out-of-shape muscles, and I was in serious danger of toppling over backwards.

Ollie must have sensed my discomfort, because he patted the ramp next to him. I straightened up with a groan and heaved my bones over there. It was cold and hard, but at least it was a seat of sorts.

It wasn't until I was sitting down that I noticed Ollie had one trouser leg rolled up past his knee. "Hey, I didn't think that look was in anymore these days."

"Huh? Oh, no. I just had a bit of an accident. Fell off my board."

"What? Let me see."

Ollie shifted around and bent his leg, hissing as he did so. "It's not that bad. Just a graze. I'm gonna need new jeans, though. Went right through the denim."

"Shit, Ollie, are you okay?" The graze looked huge, the blood glittering black in the dim glow of the distant streetlights. "You haven't sprained or broken anything, have you?"

"Nah, I'm fine."

"Then why are you sitting out here in the cold and dark all by yourself?"

"Just needed some time to think things through. About what you said. How I let Dane push me around and take advantage."

"I didn't mean to offend you. I know you're older now. You've moved on." I stopped to think of the right words to say. "I just didn't like the idea of someone like that using you. You deserve to be cherished, not treated like a servant."

"Oh." Ollie flushed and started to spin his bracelets. I stopped him by grabbing hold of his hand and holding it, rubbing my thumb over his knuckles. Ollie began quietly, hesitantly. "That was how Dane liked things to be. He worked hard all day in the office and wanted to get home to his dinner on the table, followed by a blowjob, and then he'd fuck me hard before bed. I didn't have to go out to work or do anything 'sides look after the house and be there when he wanted me. I knew where I was, then." Ollie raised his eyes, and my heart clenched at the confusion in their depths. "I don't know what you want from me. I've never had a relationship like this. I thought I could handle it, but now I'm not so sure."

"Christ, Ollie, are you serious?" It all tied in with what Zoe had told me. His urge to look after me. The way he'd taken over some of my household chores without me even realising. Ollie was used to being a kept boy and didn't know how to have any other kind of relationship. "I had no idea before today."

"No, well, I never exactly told you, did I?" Ollie gave a wry smile. "You already think I'm immature, so I reckoned I'd better keep my mouth shut about my houseboy days. Besides"—he paused to sniff and wipe his hand under his nose—"I left him because I didn't want to be treated like that anymore. I wanted to work and make my own choices like an adult. Being with Dane was like still living with my mum and stepdad, 'cept with more sex."

"*More* sex?" My mind was reeling. I wasn't sure I could cope with finding out he'd also been abused at home.

"Yeah, well, you know, when I was fourteen I used to sneak out down here at night and give the odd blowjob to my mates under the ramps, but I hadn't gone any further than that until I met Dane."

Thank God for that. "How did you meet him?" I wasn't sure I really wanted to hear all the details but I thought it might be better to get it all out now, rather than be left wondering. I huddled Ollie close to help warm us both up and wondered if we should take this conversation somewhere more comfortable. My bed, for instance. For once, the idea of having Ollie stay the night didn't fill me with fear, but I hadn't the spare attention to wonder why.

"He was manager of the firm where I did my work experience after my GCSEs. I don't reckon I was all that suited to the work, and I kept breaking the photocopier, but he took quite an interest in me. Always asking me to come to his office and help him with something that had 'come up'. Usually it was his dick. Sometimes I ended up having to hide under the desk when other people came in."

I felt sick at the thought of some aging pervert taking advantage of a nubile innocent like Ollie must have been.

Ollie continued. "As soon as I turned sixteen, Dane asked me to move in with him." Ollie smiled wistfully, and I wanted to punch this Dane fellow. "I couldn't pack my bags fast enough. And it was great, for a while. Made me feel so grown up, being the first of my friends to move out of home. The first to have a steady relationship. Then they all started going to college or getting jobs, and suddenly I was left behind. All I could talk about was daytime TV shows and doing the fucking housework. It's not like I could tell them about the sex, was it?" Ollie hugged himself, and his eyes seemed to implore me to agree.

"No." And I hoped he wasn't about to tell me about it, either. All this talk of Dane was making my fists curl. There's no way that bastard was getting any more of Ollie's attention. Ollie was with me now.

I realised how much I wanted to keep things that way.

I pulled Ollie close against my chest and spoke into the gelled spikes of his hair. "I'm sorry. I had no idea, but now I do, I can make sure things are less confusing for you. I don't want a houseboy." Ollie stiffened in my arms. "But I do want you. I want you to be independent and have your own life. I want you to open your café and draw your comics and follow your dreams, okay? And promise me you won't go running off the moment we have a disagreement. I need you to stick around and explain things so I can understand what's going on in your head."

I felt, rather than saw, Ollie's nod. His body trembled, but I didn't hear any sobs, just a sniffle, muted by him burying his damp face in the crook of my neck.

We sat like that for what felt like an age. My mind raced through ideas and emotions, trying on jealousy and anger, annoyance at Ollie for never telling me, sadness, acceptance, and finally settling on a humbling gratitude that he had chosen me, despite having such a screwy idea of what his role should be.

When he eventually pulled his face away, his eyes were dewy, but the fragile moment seemed to have passed. I could see him pulling back together that camouflage of cheeky attitude. I wanted to catch him before the naked Ollie was gone.

"Why don't you come back to mine and stay the night?" I asked, not realising that was about to come out of my mouth but rather pleased it had. "I'm not promising any action, but I'd like you to be there."

Ollie gave me a long stare, and I could see the moment when something changed in his eyes. Some part of him matured when he made the decision.

"No," he said. "Thanks, but maybe it's better if I stay a bit more independent right now. I don't want to crowd you."

I wanted to protest that he wouldn't be, but I could see the sense in his words. Maybe we had been rushing things. Maybe it was better to take a step back and wait a while, no matter what Meera said.

"I'll give you a lift back, then."

Ollie smiled and squeezed my hand.

The smell of fresh coffee tantalised my nostrils with a sweet torture. I followed temptation through to the kitchen to find that other forbidden pleasure, my delectable boyfriend, fussing over the machine as the dark, syrupy liquid trickled into his cup. I stood there for a while and watched him, wondering how long I'd be able to resist giving in to the urge to take him to my bed.

I was still reeling from Ollie's revelation a few days before. I wasn't going to be like that Dane arsehole. I wasn't going to take advantage of Ollie's youth and eagerness to please.

Hell, if I kept telling myself it often enough, I might even believe it and forget that I was also a big coward, terrified to have an orgasm in case it hurt so bad I never wanted to have sex again. I still had ten days of grace before I had no more excuses. I wondered if they'd fly by or if every moment would stretch out to taunt me.

"Mornin'," Ollie said, leaning back against the counter. As he lifted the cup to his lips, his T-shirt rode up, exposing an expanse of purple-and-green boxer shorts over the low-slung jeans, and a tantalising inch of bare flesh. I salivated.

"Was there something you wanted?" Ollie's eyes were sparkling. Bloody tease.

"Yeah." My voice came out gruff, and I tried to make it all businesslike. "I wanted to check on how things are going with the café. Are you still planning to open on the bank holiday?" Ollie's business plan had given a projected opening date at the end of May, but I knew procuring the equipment on the cheap had taken him rather longer than he'd anticipated.

"Yeah, should be. I'm gonna have to spend the next couple of weeks setting up. Decorating and sorting shit out. You won't see much of me. Zoe's gonna try and help out, but she's still working split shifts at the restaurant, so I'm not expecting much."

"That's a shame." I walked over and placed my hands on the counter on either side of him. "I'll miss you," I mumbled into his hair.

Ollie grinned and thrust his hips forward while leaning his upper body back, still balancing his espresso cup on the saucer. The rich aroma teased my nostrils, and underlying that, the scent of Ollie, sweet, dark and earthy.

"You could always come and help me," he said.

"I wouldn't be much use."

"You're strong enough to hold a paintbrush, aren't you? You could probably do most of the window frames while sitting down."

"I don't know the first thing about decorating," I admitted. Ollie gave me a disbelieving look. "I mean, I'm good at choosing the colours, but I've always got someone in to do all the work."

"Any excuse to get a sexy workman round, right?"

"Oh, yeah, any excuse."

"Hi, I'm here to paint your bedroom." Ollie imitated the hammy delivery of one of our favourite budget porn actors. "Oh, no, for some bizarre and unexplained reason, I'm wearing my best clothes. Mind if I take them off?"

I sniggered. "Go ahead. No complaints here." I hooked a finger into the waistband of his boxers and ran it across his belly.

Ollie squirmed. "Get off! I'm meant to be meeting a man with a coffee machine to sell. He didn't sound like the type who'd be too happy if I rolled in late and stinking of sex. Probably end up sticking an extra hundred on the asking price."

I pouted a little but stepped back as Ollie finished his

coffee.

"So you really can't decorate?" he asked, looking absurdly pleased with himself.

"No. Never tried."

"Excellent. Then I'm going to be able to teach you how to wield a paintbrush and roller. You can do all the boring flat stuff, and I'll have time to do the fancy bits over the top."

I groaned. "I have work to do."

He raised his eyebrows. "Thought you were meant to be taking it easy for the next few weeks."

"Well, yeah. So no decorating. It'll be too strenuous."

"It'll be good exercise. You can do it instead of letting me thrash you on the Wii."

He had me there, and he knew it. I gave a theatrical sigh.

"All right, all right. I'll let you teach me how to decorate. Happy?"

Ollie grinned. "I'll be even happier if you come with me to see this bloke about the coffee machine. Reckon I'll get a better deal with some backup. He might take me more seriously than if I rock up there on my skateboard."

I wondered exactly why it was I'd been worried about dominating Ollie. If anything, it felt like he was in the driver's seat of our relationship. Funny thing was, I enjoyed giving up the control, and he seemed to like taking it.

I tossed him my car keys on the way out. "You can drive us. I'm going to save my energy for lifting that paintbrush later."

"Are you serious?" Ollie's eyes shone. "You'll let me drive the MG? Can we have the top down?"

"It's not that warm yet," I warned, but he kept jumping on his toes like an overexcited puppy. "Oh, all right. Don't say I didn't warn you when your hair gets flattened in the breeze."

“Yes!” Ollie punched the air and bounded out the front door. I followed at a more sedate pace, pulling a hat and scarf from the stand by the door.

“What am I going to do with him?” I asked Nightcrawler as I took my front door keys from his hand. “He’s like an overexcited puppy.”

Nightcrawler just leered back. I had a feeling I knew exactly what he’d do with young Ollie.

Exactly the thing that I wanted to do with him.

# Chapter Nineteen

"Finished all the chairs!" I called out over the blaring Green Day album before falling back onto the flagstone floor with sheer exhaustion. Ollie bounced back into the main room, and I wondered again how it was possible for one man to contain so much raw energy. More to the point, I wondered how it was possible to get covered in that much paint. There I was, almost pristine in my old dialysis clothes, now relegated to decorating clothes, whereas Ollie was a rainbow of paint flecks and smears. And he'd only been painting the gents.

"Nice one!" Ollie said, grinning at the painted furniture. "That all looks brilliant. This place is gonna be amazing by the end of the week."

I sat up and panned my gaze around the room. It was fronted by a wide expanse of windows, framed in the same soft grey-green I'd just finished painting all the furniture. The room was long and narrow, but even with the counter filling up half the back wall, there was still room for a row of the previously mismatched tables and chairs to take advantage of the view. Down the other end of the room, Ollie planned to set up his kids' area and had already purchased some heavy-duty beanbags and a crate of second-hand toys. With some outdoor tables and chairs for the smokers or those catching a rare bit of British sunshine, he had the potential to seat twenty paying customers.

God knew how he was planning to cope with that many at once—more if people wanted takeaways. His cousin had agreed to help out on Saturdays and school holidays, but he'd be on his own all week during term time. I had this horrible feeling I was going to end up doing something crazy like offering to help Ollie out myself, and I didn't do sociable. Not anymore. Never had, really. The only way I got through my clubbing days was with a skinful of beer or chemicals sending their toxic courage through my system.

Ollie settled down behind me with his legs stretched out on either side. I could feel his warm breath on my earlobe and the mingled scent of sweat and chocolate wove its way around me. The sunlight falling over our legs was dappled by the fluttering leaves of the birch trees outside, and the happy shouts of kids playing sounded in the distance.

Ollie's arms wrapped around me, and euphoria dissolved through my body. Not the dizzying chemical rush of my youth but a slower, more stable happiness.

"Wotcha thinking?" Ollie murmured before kissing my neck.

"I want to help you," I said. "I want to help out. Lunchtimes, or whenever your busiest time is. I could take a few hours out of my day, at least until I go back to the office full time. Get some exercise. See you." There, it was too late to take it back.

Ollie was quiet for a long time. He wasn't trying to think of a way to let me down gently, was he? Maybe he didn't want me hanging around here. Maybe he thought I was too old and too grumpy to be any use with the customers.

"Do you really mean that?" Ollie asked.

"Of course I do," I snapped. "Wouldn't have offered

otherwise, would I?"

"No need to get all defensive. I just, I didn't have you down as the barista type. Thought you'd rather incinerate your porn collection than make tea and clean up after sticky-fingered children."

"Are you saying I'm unnaturally attached to my porn?"

Ollie laughed against my neck, and it tickled.

"I'm just saying you surprised me, that's all. Anyway, I love surprises."

"So is that a yes?"

"'Course it is, you daft sod. Why on earth would I turn you down? I'm gonna need all the help I can get for this place to work, seeing as how I'm just a dumb houseboy." Ollie's tone was teasing, but his words sliced me up inside.

I twisted round to look at him. "Don't talk crap! I mean," I added, seeing the wounded look in his eyes, "look at everything you've done with this place. That takes vision. That takes determination and hard work."

Ollie gave a secretive smile.

"What?"

"I've got another vision."

"Oh yeah?" I wasn't sure if I really wanted to know, but there was this stirring in my guts that prompted me.

"Yeah. I could draw you a picture if you like." Ollie's hand snaked down and covered the bulge at my crotch. "I've gotta warn you, I'm determined to get what I want, even if it is *hard work*." He emphasised the last two words with strokes to my cock, making it twitch and swell in response.

Shit, I wanted him. Not here, though. "Stop, someone might see." I didn't sound all that convinced, I've got to say, but as there had been passersby peering in through the windows all morning, I didn't want to risk it.

My dick begged to differ, standing to attention and demanding Ollie's touch. I swear, that thing had a mind of its own.

"I've got an idea. Hold that thought." Ollie pressed my own hand down over my erection, and I kept it there in a rather halfhearted effort at concealment, enjoying the press of my palm against needy flesh.

Ollie stood up and moved away, heading over to the pile of equipment he'd had delivered.

"What are you up to?" I demanded, seeing him lift one of the plastic-wrapped beanbags down from the stack of boxes.

"You'll see." Ollie grinned and chucked the beanbag behind the counter. I heard it land with a whisper of polystyrene beads. Then he hefted another box onto the counter. "This needs to go here anyway."

I watched, bemused, as Ollie built a wall of boxes along the countertop.

"Come on. I've built a secret love nest back here. We need to give it a trial run."

"I've still got a week to go. You know, until—"

"C'mon, Ben. Live a little."

Further protest dried up in my throat. Ollie looked so fucking sexy, leaning against the counter with his eyes like saucers and his hips thrust forward. I rose to my feet and tottered over on wobbly legs, Ollie's smile drawing me in like a lure.

I went to kiss him, but he dodged me.

"Uh-uh. I want you sitting on that. No arguments. You've done a lot today, and you need some rest and relaxation." He indicated the beanbag, still wrapped in cellophane but looking surprisingly inviting. I settled down on it with the wall supporting my back. The beads hissed around me and the surface was slippery, but I was able to get comfy.

"This beanbag's great."

"Yeah, I forked out a bit for two new ones, since I'm gonna be sleeping on them."

"You're what?"

Ollie fixed me with a level gaze. "I've got to get out of Meera and Omar's before the baby comes, and I haven't had any other offers of a place to stay."

"So you'd rather bed down on a beanbag in a cold shop?"

"I'd rather bed down with you."

He had me there. I gazed into his eyes, searching for even a trace of manipulation, but all I saw was honest desire. I thought about the prospect of falling asleep beside Ollie, of breathing in the scent of his skin, and of waking up beside him every morning. It was terrifying, but I wanted it.

"What are you frightened of?" Ollie asked. "You get this look in your eyes every time I suggest any kind of commitment."

He didn't seem pissed off—more sad than anything else. I hated seeing him like that, so I took a deep breath and gathered up the tattered rags of my courage.

"I'm scared that you'll get sick of me. You'll see me at my worst and you won't want me anymore. I don't know if I'll be able to cope if you leave me after I've got used to having you around all the time."

Ollie gave a sad smile and stroked my cheek. "Why would you think that? I think you're amazing."

"I'm not amazing. Far from it." I looked down at my hands. He'd been honest with me, and I deserved to give him the full picture of the man he wanted to hitch his fortunes to, warts and all. "I fucked up my health taking drugs, and the last guy I hooked up with died because of me."

"That's bullshit. Zoe told me it wasn't your fault."

"Zoe told you about that?" I wanted to be angry at them talking about me behind my back, but instead, I was simply relieved that he didn't seem to blame me. Maybe I could finally let go of some of the guilt I'd been clinging on to. "You know I used to be a complete arsehole, then. I just used blokes for sex. I didn't care who they were."

Ollie's eyes still gazed on me with understanding. "You were just letting off steam after being responsible for Zoe all those years. It was only to be expected."

"Honestly, I've no idea what you see in me."

His smile quirked into mischief. "You want me to give you a list?"

"It might help."

"Okay, then, you're funny and kind and patient, and I've never met anyone less arrogant in my life. You're this incredibly hot and sexy bear of a man, but you don't seem to know it." I flushed at that one and was going to interrupt, but Ollie put a finger to my lips and carried on. "You're a fantastic lover, and you take the time to make me feel incredible. You encourage me to get on and do something with my life. And the way you look at me..." Ollie looked down at the ground with a strange expression, but when he raised his gaze, his eyes were shining. "You make me feel special."

"You are special." What was I, nuts? How could I force the man I loved into sleeping on a beanbag in a cold café every night? "Ollie, will you move in with me?"

"You really mean it?"

"I mean it." I'm sure my face must have registered as much

shock as his. I hadn't been expecting to make that offer, but the moment I did, I knew it was what I wanted more than anything else.

"I'd fucking love to!" Ollie climbed onto my lap and kissed me enthusiastically, and the celebratory mood must have been infectious because before I realised what was happening, he had my trackie bottoms pooled around my ankles and my cock in his hand.

"We can't! What if someone sees?"

He gave me a tolerant smile. "No one's gonna see anything. What d'you think those boxes are for?"

I looked up at the wall he'd built and realised for the first time how private this space was. "Did you lock the door?"

"Stop trying to distract me," Ollie murmured as he bent over me. I put my hand out to stop him. "Yes! I locked the bloody door. Now, are you going to let me give you this blowjob or not, coz I've been waiting for-fucking-ever and I really, really want to do this. Please, Ben." His voice went as soft as the expression in his eyes, and I let go of his shoulder. Let him do what he wanted.

What I wanted.

The first touch of his tongue to my half-hard dick set my skin ablaze. I yelped, but a few more licks and kisses soon had me so rigid I ached. With one hand wrapped around me and applying a gentle pressure, Ollie ducked down farther and lapped my balls. A deep groan vibrated through me, and I screwed my eyes shut in embarrassment. Sounded way too pathetic and needy. Mind you, it had been, what, about a month since I'd last come? I hadn't even had a wet dream yet. Jesus, that must be some kind of record—not just for me but for any man. Especially for one with such an extensive library of masturbatory aids.

And, let's not forget, one with a horny young boyfriend who looked at him like he was a fucking hero, no matter how little he deserved it.

Ollie sucked one of my balls into his mouth with a hungry moan, and I swear I nearly shot my load then and there. My body jerked, and while there was a little stiffness in my abdomen, it didn't really hurt. Not enough to make me ask him to stop, anyway.

"Mmm, you taste amazing," Ollie said between nuzzles as he licked and nibbled a tortuously slow trail up to the tip of my dick. "All salty, like a bag of crisps."

I couldn't help it; I burst out laughing.

"What?" Ollie said, all mock innocent as he held my cock and gave a lick to the end. "Yeah, I'm getting hints of roast beef with an undercurrent of gravy. Mmm, savoury!"

"Shut up!" I wheezed, desperately trying to calm my shaking body. It still hurt to give a belly laugh, but it was worth it.

Made me think it would be worth it to have an orgasm too.

"You taste sweet," I said. "Like a mocha."

"I've got mocha spunk? Nice one! No one's ever said that before."

"No, your skin. But there might be a hint of it in your jizz, now you come to mention it. I'd have to try it again to confirm, but I think the predominant flavour is brine." I nodded sagely, doing my best impression of a wine connoisseur. I didn't want to betray the way my heart was thundering within me at the prospect of what Ollie was about to do.

"Well, I'll have to give you some tasting notes when I've finished," Ollie murmured before enveloping my cockhead in the moist heat of his mouth.

"Fu-u-u-uck!" The word shuddered out of me, and I had to reach out for Ollie's head, had to take a double handful of his vibrant, red hair. Last time it had been purple, and I had a strange sense of déjà vu, of two overlapping scenes. I remembered the way Ollie had looked at me, tube and all, with lust brimming in his eyes. As if he could read my thoughts, he moved his spare hand from my hip and found the puckered scar, gently teasing it with his fingertips. He took me deep, then eased off again and winked at me.

"Later," Ollie said.

"Huh?" I had to fight the urge to shove his head back down again.

"We'll fuck. Later. Back home."

"Okay." I sank back into the cellophane-wrapped beanbag as Ollie began to suck me off in earnest. I can't honestly say if it was his technique or the fact it was only my second blow job in more than two years, but I had to shut my eyes and concentrate on the nasty slide of the plastic under my sweaty arse to keep myself from coming too fast. But then I got to thinking about what I'd just agreed to, and the thought of sinking deep into Ollie's pert little bum set my balls boiling.

Of course, that would have to be the moment Ollie took his hand away from my dick and deep-throated me. As he swallowed around my cockhead, squeezing me tight, it was like my whole body contracted then expanded. My hips jerked, my scar throbbed, and my dick shot pulses of bright pleasure that threatened to rip me apart.

When I finally opened my eyes, still panting, still shuddering, Ollie was watching me in this weird, tender way. Like he was the elder of the two of us and I'd just impressed him by learning some new trick.

I couldn't take too much of looking into his eyes, so I

transferred my attention to his mouth and watched as a dribble of jizz escaped when he grinned.

"Messy boy," I chided, wiping it away with a trembling finger.

"You can come all over my face later if you like," Ollie offered.

"Jesus!" My head hit the wall with a painful thunk. "Yes, I do like. What are you trying to do to me?"

"Just keeping my man happy."

"Believe me, I'm happy."

"Yeah, I thought so." Ollie caressed my cheek and gave me another of those odd, tender gazes. I tried to change the subject.

"You want a hand job? Or a blowjob?" I wasn't sure I was up to either after my morning's exertions, but I'd try my best for Ollie.

"Nah, I'm good."

"Don't tell me you came in your pants."

Ollie laughed and stood up, lifting my unresisting hand to feel his erection through his jeans. "Nope. I just want to wait. I want to come in *our* bed while you're pounding my arse. I think I deserve it, don't you?"

My throat went dry, and I stared up at him, no longer able to think of a single reason why we shouldn't be at it like rabbits.

Well, except for the fact that my body seemed to have turned to jelly.

"I'll take that as a yes, then," Ollie said, then turned on his heel and strutted off. "You have a rest while I wash the brushes; then we'll stop by Omar's and pick up my stuff, okay?"

"Okay," I whispered to Ollie's retreating back.

# Chapter Twenty

When we got to Omar and Meera's place, they were both out at work, thank God, as I really didn't fancy another showdown with Mr. Macho. We'd gone straight there at Ollie's insistence. I'd tried to persuade him that the MG wasn't really a suitable moving vehicle and we should wait to hire a van, but he'd said that we'd have plenty of room. I was amazed to see how right he was when I stepped into the box room he'd had as his bedroom. There was only one narrow, high-up window, but it cast enough light to see how pitifully sparse the furnishings were.

"Is this everything you own?" I asked, unable to keep the surprise from my voice. There were a couple of piles of comics and graphic novels on the floor, a plastic toolbox full of art materials, a laptop covered in stickers, a chest of drawers stuffed full of clothes, and a few plastic spaceships hanging from the ceiling—but that was it. With no other furniture than a narrow air mattress on the floor, the room could have been depressing if it hadn't been for the brightly inked pictures all over the walls. Representations of skateboarders jostled with sketches of Cyber-Ben and Sidekick-Ollie—fortunately not the pornographic ones, though, as I didn't like the idea of his hosts clapping their eyes on those.

Ollie bustled past me with an armful of empty carrier bags.

"Yeah, this is it. Well, there's my skateboard and a couple of jackets by the front door, and I've got a mug in the kitchen, but everything else is in here. Oh, and don't worry about the airbed or the chest of drawers. Those both belong to Omar and Meera."

I felt chastened to think that Ollie'd had to come back to this joyless little cell every night when I could easily have asked him to stay at mine.

"Why don't you sit in the living room and have a rest? Won't take me a moment to pack this lot up." Ollie pulled out one of the drawers and began stuffing T-shirts haphazardly into one of the bags.

"I want to help you. I could fold those for you. They'll get all creased if you don't pack them properly." Come to think of it, they probably already were, as they looked like they'd been shoved into the drawer with the same amount of finesse.

Ollie grinned like I'd said something funny. "They're only T-shirts. Chill." He stuffed a second carrier bag with pants and socks. "Tell you what, if you want to help with something that takes a bit of care, how about you take my pictures down? You can stick 'em in here." He reached behind the chest of drawers to pull out one of those big zip-up folders the art students at school all used to have.

"Glad to be of use," I said and began gently removing the pictures from the wall. Ollie had used blu-tack, so it took real care not to pull off chunks of the paintwork as well. I studied the pictures as I worked. "We should frame these. Put them up at my place. Our place," I corrected myself, blushing.

"They wouldn't go," Ollie said in a matter-of-fact kind of way.

"Why not? This one would go perfectly with the colour scheme in the kitchen." I held up one that had caught my eye: a skater doing some kind of airborne stunt, silhouetted against a gold-and-peach sunset.

"You want my pictures up in your kitchen? Really?"

"*Our* kitchen. And yes, really. You have talent, and I want it to feel like your home too."

"Does that mean I can put my spaceships up on the bedroom ceiling?"

I cast a horrified glance up at them, imagining them hanging above the bed in my perfectly restful, harmonious bedroom.

Ollie chuckled and punched my arm. "I'm only joking. God, you should see the look on your face."

Shame washed over me. There I was, thinking of it as my bedroom still. This co-habiting was going to take some time to adjust to, I could see.

"Of course we can put your spaceships up. Just...maybe not in the bedroom. How about the living room?" I couldn't believe I'd just offered that.

"That'd be brilliant. They'll go much better with the decor in there."

I nodded, wisely deciding not to pass comment. Perhaps I'd become too precious about my interior design scheme, anyway. Who really cared if plastic spaceships knocked shoulders with Jasper Conran sofas, Italian shelving and hand-printed wallpaper? If there was room for Ollie in my life, then there was room for his stuff too. I recalled how my one touch of kitsch, the Nightcrawler key holder, had been instrumental in bringing us closer. Yes, perhaps I needed more of the quirky in my home. Let's face it, there'd be plenty of quirky with Ollie around the place.

I grabbed him around the waist and kissed him.

"What was that for?" Ollie asked.

"Just for being you."

"You're weird, you are," he said, smiling. "Now let me get on with this, yeah? I want you to take me home and fuck me stupid."

Oh yes. That. I turned back to my task and tried not to dwell on the terms "erectile dysfunction" and "performance anxiety". Unfortunately, they seemed to take up all the available room in my brain.

I lay back on my bed—our bed—wondering if this was how people used to feel on their wedding nights, back in the days when virginity was a valuable commodity. Not that I was comparing myself to a virgin bride or anything—but my poor body had been through the wars, and it had been so long since my last shag, I wasn't remotely confident I'd make a good lover.

And God, I wanted to be good for Ollie. I could hear him splashing about in the shower, singing jubilantly but slightly off key as he sluiced all that paint and sweat off his skin. We'd only got back about half an hour ago, and Ollie had dumped his bags of clothing and spaceships in the living room, promising he'd take care of them first thing in the morning. I'd taken my shower first, too weirded out about the whole moving-in thing to take him up on his offer to share, muttering some lame excuse about the stall being too small. He'd just given me another one of those affectionate looks that made me feel about five years old and said he'd switch on the heated towel rail for me.

So here I was, splayed out on the bed—our bed—the sheets smooth against my slightly damp skin. Between the soporific effect of the hot shower on my exhausted muscles and the paralysing fear that I wouldn't be able to fuck Ollie the way he deserved, I couldn't seem to be able to move. The feather duvet felt like a lead blanket pinning me to the mattress.

The clanking of the water in the pipes ceased, and my heart began to pound. It would only be moments now, and here I was, as limp as an old carrot that's been forgotten about at the back of the fridge. Bugger. I persuaded one of my arms to move and took hold of my dick. I tugged a few times, but it didn't want to wake up. Felt like the times I was full of dialysate and couldn't persuade the little bastard to respond. Not even with porn.

Now there was a thought.

I couldn't face getting up to put on a DVD, but I had Ollie's drawings in the drawer by my bed. I fumbled around and managed to grab hold of the folder with a minimum of movement, dragging it out and over. I rested a minute before opening it, aware of the sounds of Ollie towelling off, still belting out some thrash-metal tune that sounded ridiculous without the backing music.

Okay, so he'd find me looking at porn when he got back in here. What the hell? He drew it.

I pulled out the first drawing, and my breathing hitched.

It was a new one.

I was still staring at it when Ollie entered the room.

"You found it." Ollie's voice was quiet, hesitant. He gave a nervous laugh. "I was going to give that to you afterwards."

"Do you mean it?" I asked, my eyes watering like crazy.

"Yeah." Ollie lowered himself onto the edge of the bed while I gazed at the picture. It showed Cyber-Ben and Sidekick-Ollie at it again, this time with Ollie riding me. But it wasn't the erotic content that had blindsided me—it was Ollie's speech bubble. "Love you," he was saying to Ben, and the look in both their eyes was that indulgent one I'd been seeing a lot of from Ollie lately.

"You love me?" How could anyone actually love me who wasn't obliged to by blood?

"Is that okay? I mean, I thought you knew. I know it's probably way too soon, and I don't expect you to feel the same way yet, but I hoped in time you might—"

I pushed myself up and silenced him with a kiss. As our tongues slid together, a sensation of rightness washed over me. I wanted to keep doing this. With Ollie.

When we came up for air, Ollie gave me this look. "So does that mean..."

"It means I do too."

"Do what?" he asked, his cheeks dimpling.

I swallowed hard. "I think I love you."

# Chapter Twenty-One

There, that wasn't so hard after all. Okay, so my voice croaked and my palms were damp with sweat, but I'd done it. I'd said it.

And I'd meant it.

"You only think? I dunno." Ollie shook his head in mock sadness. Bugger, he was enjoying this. "Maybe it's because you haven't had a chance to do me yet. Isn't that supposed to be the moment you fall in love? When you're pumping me full of your creamy love-juice?"

I stared at him. "Have you been reading porny romance or something?"

Ollie looked shifty. "Well, I might have picked up my mum's Mills & Boons now and again. Some of the guys on the covers were pretty hot, you know?"

"You've got a taste for Fabio now, have you? I should be worried you're going to run off with some pool-cleaning hunk?"

"Nah, they're all doctors or businessmen in those books. Just like you. I reckon I'm more pool-cleaning material. Or house cleaning."

"Stop that, right now." I kissed him hard to force the issue, then took a deep breath and prepared to lay my soul bare. "You're the most mature and responsible bloke I've ever met.

You have a kind heart, and everyone loves you. You could do whatever the fuck you want with your life, and I still don't understand why you want to throw it away on a grumpy old git like me, but I feel honoured."

Ollie grinned. "You forgot something."

"What?" Damn, that speech had taken everything out of me. What more did he want?

"I have an amazingly hot and shaggable arse as well." Ollie stood up, letting the towel around his waist drop to the floor so he could illustrate the point.

I reached out to squeeze one of those tempting buttocks. "Oh yeah. So you do." Energy buzzed through me, reviving my exhausted muscles, and I sat up properly, swinging my legs down over the edge of the bed. A line came to mind from that DVD he'd brought round, and I grinned. Hopefully Ollie would get the reference.

"Put your hands against the wall and spread 'em, punk."

Ollie gave a delighted gasp, and I felt a jolt pass through his body. He leant forward to comply, walking his hands down the mirror on the wardrobe door so that his arse was raised in welcome.

"Officer, you won't force the truth out of me like this," he protested, shooting me a look over his shoulder that was pure mischief. "No matter how hard you beat me with your love truncheon." Yeah, he fancied himself as the twink hoodlum, caught by the big bad bear of a cop. Shame I didn't have the hat. Or the uniform.

But the role-playing was only a distraction, something to take my mind off the bewildering confession Ollie had made, and to combat my performance anxieties. And I didn't need to pretend to be a horny policeman to do that. I only had to reach out and part Ollie's cheeks, bend down and taste him.

The yelp Ollie made when my tongue teased his hole was like nothing I'd ever heard from him before, and his hips jerked so hard I nearly sprained my neck trying to keep contact.

"God, keep still, will you? I'm trying to rim you here."

"Yeah. I…I can tell. Oh fuck, that's so m-much more…"

"So much more what?" I teased, insanely flattered that I'd reduced him to incoherency. I'd had no idea a simple rim job would do that to him. Should have tried it sooner, really, but as he'd never illustrated one or passed comment while they were rimming on the DVDs, I'd assumed he wasn't all that into them. From his reaction, though, I started to think maybe it was just that he'd never experienced one before.

"Just, God, do it again, will you? C'mon, Ben!"

I couldn't resist him, this man I loved, so I gave a few long licks from his balls up to his hole, before sealing my lips around his entrance and sucking. I'm glad I kept a firm grip on his hips because that had him bucking again, pulling away from me and making a peculiar gurgling noise.

"You okay?" I asked when I heard his head hit the wardrobe, making the hangers inside rattle.

"Yes! It just…it feels so dirty."

"In a good way?"

"Fuck yes!" Ollie's tone was emphatic enough to leave me in no doubt that he was enjoying himself. I gave a quick manual check and discovered he was as hard as I was, and I was like bloody granite at that point.

I made my voice extra deep and gravelly. "Just you wait till you feel my tongue in there."

Ollie groaned, and I pushed my advantage, pulling his cheeks as far apart as they'd go and relentlessly swirling my tongue around and over his puckered hole. I waited until he was swearing nonsense words and his legs were trembling before breaching him. He was hot and tight, his flavour heady and intense. I growled as I plunged in eagerly, desperate for more.

"Ben! Oh fuck, I can't stop!"

I felt Ollie's muscles contract around me as his body stiffened. It might have been my imagination as the howl he gave just about split my eardrums, but I swear I heard his jizz hit the mirror with a satisfying splatter.

"I'm so sorry," Ollie panted.

"No need to be." I kissed his tailbone, wincing a little at the ache in my jaw. "You're young. You'll get it up again soon enough."

"No, I mean, I've just spunked all over your slippers."

We both looked down at the jizz-soaked monster feet. I started to snigger, but Ollie gave me this wounded look in the mirror.

"I don't even know if you can put those in the washing machine. They might be dry-clean only."

"Ollie, I really don't give a shit about the slippers. I'll either wear them spunky or buy a new pair. Now stop worrying about it, and come and lie down with me."

When we were snuggled up together, Ollie's head nestled under my chin and his legs tangled up in mine, I broached the question.

"So no one's ever done that for you before, then?"

He tensed slightly, then sighed and relaxed against me.

"No. Never. I always thought it might be a bit, uh, disgusting." I could feel Ollie grimace against my skin.

"Disgusting?" I tried to wrap my head around what could be disgusting about eating a guy out. "What, like, immoral or something?"

"No! You know. Did I...did I taste all right?" Ollie buried his face even farther into my shoulder so his words came out all muffled, but I could still hear the vulnerability lurking there.

I shifted a little, pulling his head back so I could look him in the eyes. "You tasted absolutely delicious, and I can prove it." I kissed Ollie deeply, enjoying the surprised moan that escaped him as my tongue delved into his mouth. He kissed me back enthusiastically, and I was pleased to feel his prick firming up again as he writhed against me. Oh, the joys of being twenty!

"See what I mean," I said when I eventually broke the kiss.

"Mmm, yeah. Might have to give it a try on you. But not right now," Ollie added, rutting against my leg. "Right now, you owe me a shag."

"Oh yeah. Look, Ollie..." He gave me this quizzical look as I trailed off, and I had to remind myself that he'd just shown me his vulnerable side. If I couldn't trust him and—quite literally—expose my soft underbelly, then what chance did we really have of making this thing work? "I hope you're not expecting too much from me. I'll do my best, but I'm still fairly weak, and all that painting knackered me out, so I think you'll have to do most of the—"

"I know all that, dumbarse." Ollie gave one of those indulgent smiles again. "Is that what you've been getting all worked up about all this time? Why don't you just lie on your back, and I'll take care of us, yeah?"

I stared into his kind eyes and rolled onto my back. I was painfully aware that my dick had softened again, and I hoped Ollie could persuade the little traitor to play along. "There's stuff in the drawer," I muttered.

"Should I check the best-before?" Ollie teased. "Make sure they're not out of date after all those years of self-inflicted celibacy?"

"Oi! I bought those last week."

"Oh, so you've been planning this seduction, have you? And there was me thinking you were trying to wriggle out of it."

"Shut up," I said and stopped his mouth with a kiss.

It took a while for me to get back to full hardness, but Ollie's fingers stroked and squeezed just so as he kissed my lips. I probably would've asked for a blowjob if I'd been able to get a word out, but he wouldn't stop kissing, and that was all right by me too.

Actually, that was bloody incredible.

But eventually he broke it off, and by then I was ready for him. Ready for the latex rolling down my shaft and the cool drizzle of lube. Ready to watch Ollie straddle me and finger himself, concentration and horniness warring on his face.

Ready to face my fears.

I think time must have stopped for a moment when Ollie lined himself up. It seemed like I had an age to study him there: the floppy mess of his freshly washed hair, the warmth in his eyes, the flush tinting his kiss-swollen lips, the tight cords of his muscles as he held himself there, waiting, I realised, for some signal from me. I could have watched him like that for longer, but I wanted to see how that beatific expression changed as he took me into him.

I nodded.

Ollie flashed me a quick grin and began to move. Tight heat squeezed the head of my cock, and I gasped, but Ollie just laughed. I could feel his muscles working to pull me inside, and sooner than I was prepared for, I felt his arse grind against me. I was enveloped in delicious pressure and totally at his mercy.

"Shiiiit!" I hissed, trying to get my breathing back under

control.

Ollie gave a breathless chuckle, and I looked up into his face. His cheeks were a little flushed, his pupils dilated, and his lips curved in a smug grin. God, he had me right where he wanted me, didn't he?

I found I didn't mind one bit.

"How's that?" Ollie asked. "Comfortable?"

"Comfortable isn't the right word."

Ollie frowned. "D'you need me to move? Maybe try it lying on our sides?"

"No! I want to see your face. This is fine, more than fine. It's just...it's too fucking intense for me to call it comfortable."

Understanding dawned with a smile that felt like warm syrup had just been poured over my heart. "Yeah," Ollie breathed. "I want to watch your face too. And be able to do this." He leaned down and pressed a kiss to my lips. His movement created a delicious friction around my cock, and I realised just how ready I was for this. Even the press of his dick against the tube and my scar didn't bother me. In fact, I enjoyed the sensation of him leaving moist trails of precome against my skin.

I raised my hands to Ollie's hips and wordlessly encouraged him to start moving, kissing him fiercely and trying to let him know just how much I needed this. He began slowly, not raising himself off me at all, but undulating his body, circling his hips and doing something clever with his muscles so that my dick received the most incredible massage. I don't know how long he kept it up as Ollie was so hot in bed, time melted around us.

Ollie moaned into my mouth. Not one of the theatrical, porn star moans he made while tossing one off to a DVD, but more of a surprised sound. Heartfelt. I broke the kiss.

"I love you," I said.

"You're only saying that 'coz you're balls deep in my arse." Ollie seemed to be trying for humour, but I wasn't laughing.

"Bollocks. I love you, and you'd better believe it or else."

"Good. Quite right too."

Ollie's eyes were looking suspiciously bright, and my own felt prickly, but I was buggered if I was going to get all teary in the middle of our first shag. "C'mon, then, get moving. I'm bloody knackered, I am."

"Can I really stay tonight?" Ollie blinked and sniffed. "Promise me this isn't a dream. I don't wanna wake up back on that airbed."

"'Course you can. This is your home now." I ran my hands up and down his sides, marvelling that this lithe and sexy young man wanted to throw his lot in with a lumbering old bear like me. Still, there's no accounting for tastes, I suppose. You should see some of the special-interest DVDs there are out there.

Then Ollie distracted me by lifting himself up and plunging down onto me, and if I hadn't been so thoroughly in love, I'd have been humiliated by the squealy grunt that escaped me. But there wasn't time for any more thought. No time for anything but the sensation of Ollie riding my dick like he was born to do it, gyrating his hips in a way that enhanced the sensations as he rose and fell. His prick and balls slapped against my stomach with every down stroke until I let go of his hips and took hold of his shaft with one sweaty hand, cupping his balls with the other. Ollie's needy, incoherent pleas spurred me on, and I lifted my hips a little, managing a few shallow thrusts.

"Oh fuck! Ben, that's it. That's it. Yes!" Ollie hissed, arching his back, and I felt his cock throb as he shot plumes of jizz all over my chest and belly. One drop even splashed against my chin, and I managed to lick it off, flooding my mouth with his rich flavour. The pungent scent of sex, the taste of him on my tongue, the heat of him clenching around me, Ollie's whimpers and the sight of him, all debauched and flushed—well, it all combined to make my nuts feel fit to burst. I shot into him, again and again, catching the same wave of pleasure Ollie was riding and following him to the distant shore.

I fell asleep in his arms, his sweat-sticky body plastered to my own.

# Chapter Twenty-Two

The Melon Grab was starting to get busy when I turned up for my first shift, the Saturday before the bank holiday. I'd been surprised by the wholesome, healthy-sounding name, but Ollie said it was the name of a skateboarding trick, so it seemed appropriate. I'd wanted to accompany Ollie in that morning, but he'd insisted I stay behind and let him open up by himself. I think he wanted to feel independent. It was surprising how quickly I'd become used to his presence in the flat—he'd moved in five days ago, and already I couldn't remember how I'd managed without him. Not that I was relying on him to do everything for me or anything—far from it. I'd been bringing him breakfast in bed every morning—but without him, the place felt strangely empty, my footsteps echoing disconcertingly.

So it was a relief to see his beaming face as I walked into the café. Things were quiet, with just a couple of teenagers sharing a table outside and a table of mums chatting, babes in arms.

"How's it going?" I asked. "Been busy?"

"Busy enough to keep me on my toes. Why don't you sit down for a moment. Rest before you start working."

"I'm fine. It was a nice walk."

"Yeah, I know you're fine, but I think you'll feel even better once you've had a drink, and you know what day it is, don't you?"

I racked my brain. What had I missed in our week of chaos as Ollie simultaneously moved house, got the café ready for opening and shagged all the stuffing out of me? "Tell me it's not your birthday, because I haven't got you a present yet."

"It's not my birthday. I can't believe you don't remember after all that fuss you've been making about your diet sheets."

"Oh my God, it's Food Day!" I'd forgotten to even look at the damn sheets that morning. Today I had full permission to indulge in all those things that had been forbidden for so long. Today I got to put my new pancreas and kidney through their paces and dose them with sugar, caffeine and even alcohol. Well, maybe not all at once. I didn't want them to give up on me in disgust.

"Yep, Happy Food Day to you. So, what's it going to be? An espresso? I have caramel and almond syrup, if you fancy it. Or I could do a latte or a hot chocolate or a—"

"Mocha," we said together and laughed.

"Mocha it is, then."

I sat on the bar stool and watched Ollie operate the coffee machine, admiring the economical way he moved while packing the filter holder and frothing the milk. He looked good in the black apron too, and I noted the way it parted at the back, revealing a tasty glimpse of a denim-clad arse and a flash of bright red polka-dot boxers sticking out the top. I still wasn't quite used to his new shade of Bahama-blue hair dye, but it would probably grow on me by the time he decided to change the colour again. At least the dark roots were growing through now, which made it a little less startling than the red had been when I first saw it.

I panned my gaze around the café, taking in the pictures we'd hung on the walls together. Ollie had refused at first, saying he didn't have the budget to buy decent frames for his drawings, but I'd made them my congratulatory present to him. They looked amazing professionally mounted and framed, and I'd even persuaded him to put prices on them in case anyone wanted to buy them. I thought he was underselling himself with the amounts he'd put on the stickers, but he'd insisted, claiming he'd have far more chance of making a sale if he didn't price himself out of the market. That was Ollie for you. No point trying to change his mind about something once he'd made a decision.

Ollie placed the cup in front of me with a flourish. "It'd be nice to put some rum in there too, but you'll have to wait until we get home as I don't want to get closed down by the police."

"This is perfect how it is, cheers." I bathed my face in the mouth-watering steam and admired the swirling design he'd somehow created in the top by pouring the milk cleverly. "Shit, you're really good at this, aren't you? I hope you're not expecting my coffees to come out this good."

"If you think I'm letting you anywhere near Bertha, you've got another thing coming."

"Bertha?"

"Big Bertha, my coffee machine. I'm her jealous boyfriend, and she ain't gonna be touched by no one but me." Ollie gave a threatening scowl before his grin twitched back into place. "Sorry, Ben, but you'll have to work your way up to making coffees. No exceptions just because you're screwing the boss."

I nearly spluttered on my first mouthful when he said that, but managed to swallow it down, looking around hastily to see if anyone had been listening in. The mums were all still chatting away, the teenagers outside flicking bits of paper at each other.

"I'm out, Ben. It's no big deal. I thought you were too."

"Yes, I am. It's just, er, been a while. Fuck. Sorry, I'm

totally out of practice."

"Oh, I wouldn't say that." Ollie waggled his eyebrows salaciously. "You've been getting a fair bit of practice this last week."

Then he took my hand, right in front of everyone, and held it there on the counter. I took another sip of mocha to steady my nerves. Caffeine jolted through my system as the flavour melted across my tongue. I closed my eyes and moaned with pleasure, opening them again to find Ollie smirking at me. "This is amazing. Not just the coffee. Everything. The café." I looked down at our interlinked fingers. "You..."

"I know, I know. The way to a man's heart is through his stomach. You'll say anything now." Something sparked in Ollie's eyes. "So, d'you still think I taste like mocha, now you've tried the real thing again?"

I took another sip of the velvety thick liquid, moaning deliberately and licking my lips once I'd swallowed. Ollie looked like he was enjoying the show, watching my lips with dark eyes.

"Mmm, there's no comparison really."

"No?" He raised his eyebrows.

"No." I leaned across the counter and kissed him briefly. "This is delicious, but you taste divine."

Ollie beamed. "Charmer. You're still on washing-up duty, though."

I scooped up a gobbet of milk foam and dotted it on the end of his nose.

"Suits me just fine."

I kissed him again.

# About the Author

English through and through, Josephine Myles is addicted to tea and busy cultivating a reputation for eccentricity. She writes gay erotica and romance but finds the erotica keeps cuddling up to the romance, and the romance keeps corrupting the erotica. She blames her rebellious muse, but he never listens to her anyway, no matter how much she threatens him with a big stick. She's beginning to suspect he enjoys it.

Visit josephinemyles.com for more about her published stories, saucy free reads and regular blog posts.

*Enjoy the following excerpt from* Barging In…

Robin caught Dan's eye, and it was like he'd been captured by the current, pulled in against his will. It wasn't fair. Someone like Dan shouldn't have eyes that beautiful. He was mesmerised by the flecks of green and amber and that band of ginger freckles sprinkled across the bridge of his nose.

And then, before Robin could say anything else, Dan pulled him into a kiss. His lips pressed hot and soft against Robin's. Perhaps it was the effect of the pint he'd just had on an empty stomach; perhaps it was the sweet, musky scent rising from Dan's body; or perhaps it was simply the relief of being saved from Charles's advances. Whatever it was, against his better judgment Robin sank into the kiss, parting his lips and clutching Dan to him with greedy arms.

Dan slid his tongue into Robin's mouth and made a delightful discovery. Not only did Robin have rings through his nipples, but there was a barbell through his tongue as well. Dan moaned as the metal ball made contact with his palate, his tongue. There was a tiny click every time it clashed against his teeth. God, he wanted that hot mouth around his dick so fucking badly. It had been a while since he'd had head from a bloke with a pierced tongue. Wonder if he had piercings anywhere more intimate?

He stretched on his toes to deepen the kiss, wound his arms around Robin's neck and pressed against him, body to body. Robin must be able to feel how much he wanted him, what with the way his prick was starting to harden and rub against Robin's thigh. He rocked his hips to emphasise the point.

Robin froze and started to pull back from the kiss.

Dan thought fast. He couldn't lose his advantage now. Not when he had Robin exactly where he wanted him. He sank back onto his heels, gave his sultriest smile and took one of Robin's unresisting hands, lacing their fingers together.

"Come on, gorgeous, we're running late." He tugged Robin after him and headed for the door, turning to call back to the old geezer with the Robin fixation. "Thanks for looking after him for me. He gets into all sorts of trouble when I'm not there to keep an eye on him."

The pub door swung shut behind them. Dan led Robin around the corner and found a large pillar in the shadows outside a closed shop to push him up against. Robin was still dazed, his eyes hooded and his jaw slack. Yeah, that had been a great kiss. Guys were always telling him he had a talented tongue, and seeing what it had done to Robin made him swell with pride. He dropped his hands to Robin's hips and purred seductively.

"Now, where were we?"

Robin made an alarmed sound in his throat and pulled back slightly, his body trembling. Dan gave a delighted smile. Surely the big guy wasn't out of his depth, was he? But yes, fear lurked in his eyes.

"No need to worry, you're in safe hands. I've done this plenty of times before."

It was as if the words broke the spell his kiss had cast. Robin's eyes widened, and his body stiffened, but not in the place Dan wanted it to.

"How many times?"

"What?"

"How many times have you done *this* before?" Robin

snarled, pushing Dan away with a shove to his chest. “You make a habit of picking up strange men, do you?”

Oh God, it was back to Mr. Shouty again, was it? “You’re not that strange. I even know your surname, which is more than I do with some guys.” He’d been aiming for light banter, but the disgust on Robin’s face made him realise he’d misjudged. Dan backpedalled. “I dunno, you just seemed like you needed a hand, and I knew I owed you one, and then I couldn’t help myself, you looked so delicious.”

“Yeah, well... I was doing fine by myself, thank you very much.”

“Didn’t look like it from where I was standing. You looked like you were struggling with how to let the guy down without being rude. That’s always a recipe for disaster. Best to be honest and get it all out in the open.” Dan grinned, but it didn’t seem to make an impression on his quarry.

“What makes you think I wasn’t interested in him? I suppose someone like you wouldn’t shag an old queen like him if he were the last man on earth, although you’d quite happily work your way through every sleazy little whore at a place like the Hussars.” Robin’s lip curled up in a sneer.

“Look, I’m not a one-man kind of bloke, and I don’t see why I should be ashamed of that.” Dan stuck out his chin. He was buggered if he was going to let Robin take the moral high ground here. “I’m a player.”

“You’re a slut, you mean.”

“Fuck you.”

“Not a chance. I’ve got a girlfriend anyway. Mel. You remember?” There was no mistaking the challenge in Robin’s eyes. It was that defensiveness that fundamentally honest people always betrayed when they were lying through their teeth. “I’d better get going. I’m supposed to be meeting her at the Hat and Feather."

Dan wasn't going to let him get away that easily. "Funny that, I figured you were gay, the way you kissed me back in the pub. The *gay* pub, where you were having a drink with a *gay* man." Bloody hell, if that wasn't a blush spreading across Robin's cheeks and making him look even more edible.

"I'm bi, but that's nobody's fucking business but my own, okay? Not that it matters, anyway, because I'm off to see my girlfriend. Good-bye, Dan." His voice was sharp enough to make Dan wince, and it deterred him from following after Robin as he stalked away.

"See you soon, Robin," he called.

Robin didn't turn back.

Sighing heavily, Dan wrapped his jacket closer around his body and headed off towards the Hussars. Robin was right; that probably was more his kind of place, and there was no point wasting the evening. There'd be plenty of opportunity to get to work on Robin before he had to go back to London. He'd have him by the time his trip was over.

A smirk tugged at his lips.

Robin wouldn't know what had hit him. Dan was going to rock his world.

*Enjoy the following excerpt from* Wight Mischief...

Feeling with his toes for his flip-flops, which had disappeared somewhere under his desk apparently of their own accord, Marcus shut down his computer. Slip-slapping into the hall, he grabbed his Maglite and keys.

Halfway from the house to the tunnel entrance—his own private shortcut to the beach—Marcus started to wonder if this was such a good idea. On cue, the security light on the house clicked off, leaving him in darkness. Marcus quickly switched on his Maglite to cover the last ten yards.

The light at the tunnel entrance didn't come on until he was almost upon it—Marcus had had it adjusted that way on purpose. He rather liked the idea of the tunnel being hidden this end unless you knew it was there. Not much he could do about the other end, thirty feet of aluminium staircase being rather hard to miss, but then there was no reason anyone should be on his property in the first place.

Of course, that hadn't stopped them last night. Marcus's feet skidded nervously on the loose chalk as he entered the tunnel. He cursed. It was his beach—why the hell shouldn't he go for a midnight walk? This time, though, the clothes were staying on. If there *had* been someone there last night, and if he happened to turn up tonight in the hopes that the Marcus Devereux strip show was playing all week, he was in for a big disappointment. Followed by a prosecution for trespass.

Reaching the lower end of the tunnel, Marcus unlocked the gate and switched off his Maglite, preferring to let his eyes adjust to the moonlight as soon as possible. Wrapping his arms around himself, he picked his way down the metal staircase toward the sand, his light tread and rubber-soled flip-flops making his steps almost silent. He halted abruptly as he realised there *was* someone there.

He was down by the water's edge, in a pair of baggy shorts that ended at the tops of his well-muscled calves. Marcus could make out a bulky shape that must be his shoes slung over one impossibly broad shoulder. The man was just standing there, staring out to sea. As if he was waiting for someone. As the turning tide lapped against his ankles, Marcus shivered in sympathy. Then recalled this was, in all probability, the man who'd made him throw himself into the icy water only last night.

Why was he here again? Did he hope to see Marcus—or any other naked men; after all, there was nothing to indicate he was particularly choosy—or did he just like the beach? *My* beach, he reminded himself angrily.

Could this be Barrie? He'd sounded like a young man on the phone. And it would certainly make sense—he was probably hoping for a glimpse of the ghost, or at least a bit of atmosphere to add colour to a report of its non-appearance.

It must have been he who'd startled Marcus the previous evening. Marcus ought to feel outraged, he knew—but there was just something about the man at the water's edge that seemed to make Marcus keen to forgive. Something apologetic about his posture, as if he knew he shouldn't be here but couldn't stay away. Marcus was suddenly seized with an absolute *need* to see the man's face. Should he approach him?

What would he say, though? This man had seen him *naked* last night.

*And he's still come back here again.* Marcus could almost hear the thought. It sounded so loud in his head that for a moment, he thought Barrie (if it was him) must hear it too.

Nobody had seen Marcus completely naked since he was a

small child. He'd always thought—but maybe he'd been wrong? Maybe, in all the infinite variety of human sexuality, there was somebody who wouldn't find him physically repulsive? Even when sober?

He was being ridiculous—and even if he wasn't, he'd still manage to bollocks it all up the minute he opened his mouth. He just didn't do people. Leif was right—he was better off staying alone.

That way, he wouldn't get hurt. Marcus turned, and headed silently up the stairs once more.

Will sighed. His feet had gone numb in the icy seawater, and he desperately needed to pee. And although he was all alone here, sod's law if he did start having a slash that'd be the precise moment the ghost turned up, probably to wreak terrible vengeance on him for daring to pollute the water. He really didn't like to think just what sort of vengeance might spring to mind to a spirit who saw him with his tackle out.

As he made his way back over the sand, for a moment he stilled, thinking he'd seen something out of the corner of his eye. But the movement didn't repeat itself and the calls of his bladder were getting urgent, so Will climbed back over the rickety fence and headed back to camp, making a pit stop en route once he was well away from the private land.

When he got back to the tent, there was a light glowing inside. Will stopped a minute, trying to work out if Baz was alone in there. At last deciding that if Baz did have a girl with him, she was bloody small and unusually quiet, he lifted the flap.

"Finally! Where the hell have you been all this time? I was about to start without you!" Baz lay there on top of his sleeping bag, starkers. His prick, Will couldn't help but notice, was half-hard and stiffening by the minute.

Will swallowed. "What happened to Courts?"

"Buggered if I care. Haven't seen her since this morning. Haven't wanted to, come to that. Worst blowjob I ever had." Baz smiled lazily, his head cradled in his hands. "No one gives head like you do, Fish. Unless you've forgotten how to do it?" His voice was low and sultry.

His mouth suddenly dry, Will shook his head slowly. He didn't trust himself to try to speak. God, Baz was gorgeous. He could be the bloody poster boy for "small but perfectly formed". And that smile of his... Will jerked off sometimes just thinking of that smile.

Realising he was just kneeling there at the entrance to the tent like an idiot, Will scrambled in and pulled off his shirt.

"That's better," Baz whispered. "Now the rest of it."

Will's hands shook as he fumbled with the button of his board shorts. He wrenched them off along with his underwear and clambered over his friend's body.

"You can kiss me," Baz said generously. He didn't always go for that.

Will wasn't going to wait for him to change his mind. He moaned as he covered Baz's body with his own, their hard pricks brushing together. Baz tasted of beer and burnt food, and his lips were rough beneath Will's, bruising. Their tongues twined briefly, and then Will felt hands on his head, pushing him down. He went eagerly, kissing his way down Baz's slender, perfect chest. He tried to pause at Baz's belly button, to tease a little with his tongue, but Baz wasn't having any of it. Those hands in his hair increased their pressure, so Will went with it, all the way down to Baz's straining cock.

God, he tasted good. Like earth and sea air. Will wondered

for a moment whether Courts had savoured it like he did, then angrily tried to banish her from his mind. She was history. Will licked a slow trail up the length of Baz's cock, then circled the head with his tongue.

"Fuck!" Baz gasped.